Famous
Last
Words

Famous Last Words

Jennifer Salvato Doktorski

Christy Ottaviano Books

Henry Holt and Company

NEW YORK

Henry Holt and Company, LLC
Publishers since 1866
175 Fifth Avenue
New York, New York 10010
macteenbooks.com

Library of Congress Cataloging-in-Publication Data
Doktorski, Jennifer Salvato.
Famous last words / Jennifer Salvato Doktorski.—First
edition.
pages   cm
"Christy Ottaviano Books."
Summary: During a summer internship as an obituary
writer for her local northern New Jersey newspaper,
sixteen-year-old Samantha D'Angelo makes some
momentous realizations about politics, ethics, her
family, romance, and most important—herself.
ISBN 978-0-8050-9367-4 (hardcover)
ISBN 978-0-8050-9840-2 (e-book)
[1. Newspapers—Fiction.   2. Journalism—
Fiction.   3. Self-perception—Fiction.   4. Dating
(Social customs)—Fiction.   5. Internship
programs—Fiction.]   I. Title.
PZ7.D69744Fam 2013   [Fic]—dc23   2012046312

Henry Holt books may be purchased for business or
promotional use. For information on bulk purchases,
please contact Macmillan Corporate and Premium
Sales Department at (800) 221-7945 x5422 or by
e-mail at specialmarkets@macmillan.com.

First Edition—2013/Designed by Ashley Halsey
Printed in the United States of America

10 9 8 7 6 5 4 3 2 1

For Mike, my AJ, and Carley, my heart.
I love you both to the edge of the universe and
back a kazillion times.

chapter one

The Obit Page

Samantha Elisabeth D'Angelo, the *Herald Tribune*'s youngest-ever obituary writer, died Friday. She was 16. Born and raised in Chestnutville, New Jersey, D'Angelo would have been a senior at Chestnutville High School in September. She is survived by her fabulous-looking and infinitely cooler mother and father, Christina and David D'Angelo, and her quirky grandmother, Alfonsina D'Angelo. A funeral mass will be held Saturday at 9:00 a.m. at St. Rose of Lima Church. In lieu of flowers, donations may be made to Snore, the D'Angelo family foundation for other extraordinarily boring high school students whose lives are so dull, they make up their own obituaries.

'm not dead. But sometimes I feel like I might as well be.

I stare at my computer screen one second more

before quickly highlighting select all and hitting delete. I don't want Bernadette, the copy-desk editor, to catch me screwing around with my own fake obituary when I should be working. My second day here, she dubbed me the bane of her existence because of my atrocious spelling. I'm now halfway through my third week, and our relationship hasn't improved. Not even a smidge.

"How many obits we got so far?" asks AJ Bartello, the college intern who has been training me since the beginning of June.

"Only seven," I tell him.

We're having a slow day.

"If we don't double that number soon, Bernie is going to make us write a freakin' feature," he says.

At nineteen, AJ is a two-year veteran of the obit desk and has earned the right to call our boss Bernie. She told me, however, that I must address her as Bernadette.

"Not another feature. I can't make the so-how-did-you-feel-about-your-dead-husband phone call again," I say.

Standard obits include the same basic information in the same order. Name, age, hometown, date of death, survivors, and services. But on days when there aren't enough regular obits to fill the page, Bernadette picks the standout death du jour for a feature. That means we have to call a surviving family member, chat about the deceased, and gather enough interesting quotes to write a lengthy profile, complete with a photo. Yesterday, I made the mistake of asking her why we couldn't fill the space with some famous person's obit, someone outside our coverage area.

"Can't we run an AP story?" I asked Bernie.

What good is having an international news-gathering agency at our disposal if we don't use Associated Press wire copy on the obit page?

Bernie was irritated by my question. "AP reporters already know how to gather news. Their well-documented expertise dates back to the Mexican War," Bernie said with a less-than-hospitable southern accent. "You're here to *learn* something."

So far, what I've learned is that most people are not feature-obit material. Take me, for instance. My life is definitely lacking superlatives. At school, I'm not the head cheerleader or class slut or teacher's pet. Just one of the nobodies who will graduate in approximately twelve months *without* a special mention in the yearbook. I'm going to be seventeen at the end of the summer, and nothing big has ever happened to me. I've never tried illicit substances, engaged in premarital anything, or attended a prom. I don't have a driver's license yet, and I still sleep with a night-light. But if I keel over while I'm working here, I'd finally have some real headline potential: SAMANTHA D'ANGELO, THE *HERALD TRIBUNE*'S YOUNGEST OBIT WRITER, DEAD.

I glance at the clock in the corner of my computer screen. It's already 3:15 p.m. Bernadette usually makes the feature call by 4:00.

4

"Moronica!" she yells across the newsroom. Damn. Bernadette's not wasting any time today.

"She's using the feminine," AJ says without looking up from his terminal. "She means you."

Harry Walters, the editor in chief, may be the big boss at the newspaper, but clearly, Bernadette is the boss of me.

"Does she call everyone Moron or Moronica, or just the people she doesn't like?" I ask.

"For Bernie, it's all the same. She doesn't like people. She's a riot during our annual sensitivity training," AJ says.

"And she just gets away with it?"

AJ peers at me through glasses so ugly, they're cool.

"She's been here for, like, a hundred years. I don't think Harry has the heart to fire her. Maybe he thinks she'll just keep coming in anyway, like Bartleby. It's like she holds up that wall behind her," he says.

I glance over at Bernie/Bernadette, who's inhaling a supersize meal. With spiky champagne blond hair and a substantial belly, she's Heat Miser meets Ursula the sea witch.

"She's certainly big enough. It wouldn't kill her to lay off the fries," I blurt out before covering my mouth.

I hope only AJ heard me. My inner monologue has been slipping out lately. I have to admit, though, it feels pretty good.

"Moronica!" Bernadette says again. "How many?"

Lucky for Bernadette, I also have an inner *censor*.

"Seven!" I yell.

"That's not going to cut it. Come over here and give me a rundown."

Crap, crap, crap, crap, crap, my mind screams. I take the ponytail holder off my wrist and pull my long, brown, style-resistant hair into a messy twist before heading over to the copy desk. I cut through the Nerf basketball court behind me, swing around the group of desks that serves as the features department, and arrive at her corner desk.

"Read me the list," she says, only half looking up as she alternates between editing copy and taking bites of a greasy burger.

"Um, civil engineer, teacher, homemaker, pastry chef," I say.

"Stop! The pastry chef—male or female?"

"Male. Does it matter?"

"Not really. Where did he work?"

"The Waldorf Astoria."

"Let's do him," she says. "Call the funeral home and get a number for the family."

"Okay," I say, afraid to argue that we still have a couple of hours and some more obits might come in.

Even though I get a byline, it doesn't compensate for the stomach pains that accompany merely thinking about writing feature obits. This probably sounds pretty bad, but I keep hoping more people in our northern New Jersey coverage area will die. Not a lot of people. Just enough to fill the darn obit page. Before I started working here, I got nervous every time I called Vinnie's Pizzeria to place an order. Now I phone grieving families on a daily basis. It's like I've been living my life in dog years.

As I recross the Nerf court, Harry bounces the orange ball off the back of my head.

"Still here, D'Angelo?" he asks. "I thought Bernie would have broken you by now. You've written a record number of feature obits since you started. Must be your name. People don't seem to die when you're at the obit desk."

As I slink over to my seat, Harry starts singing "Hark, the Herald D'Angelo Sings" as he takes a jump shot. Lean, with unruly black hair and a goatee that's turning gray, Harry looks more like an aging 1970s rock star than an editor.

I sigh and reach for my desk phone just as my cell vibrates in my pocket. I replace the receiver on its cradle and sneak a glance at my phone's screen: a new text message. I'm sure it's from my friend, Shelby. We haven't been getting along so well lately, and I'm choosing to blame her. Apparently, prompted by the excessive consumption of Mike's Hard Lemonade at a party in early June, she strutted (or maybe staggered) up to the most popular guy in our class, Rob McGinty, and confessed *my* longtime crush on him.

Ever since then, my bestie has been calling me relentlessly and begging forgiveness. Not only am I angry about her newfound party-girl ways, I'm pissed about how her drinking is affecting me. Rob lives in my neighborhood.

What if I run into him? What about when school starts again? He has a *girlfriend*.

"You're scowling," AJ says, interrupting the cloud of fury building in my head.

"Am not," I say. Now I'm a defensive first grader.

"Don't worry. Harry likes you," AJ says.

"How can you tell?" I ask. I don't bother to correct his misread of my scowl.

"He talks to you," AJ says. "You're on his good side. I'd try to stay there if I were you."

"Why? Is his bad side that bad?" I ask. I ignore a second text from Shelby. I can't deal with her neediness right now.

"Bernie's annoying but harmless. Harry goes *off*. We really need to keep one of those tranquilizer guns around here. You know, like the kind they use for rabid animals?"

"So far, he just seems a little goofy to me," I say.

"Goofy? Where do you get *goofy*?"

"Oh, I don't know, maybe that collection of windup toys he keeps on his desk, next to his Rock 'Em Sock 'Em Robots?"

"Good point."

"And when he hired me, he told me to put my palms flat on the desk. Then he whipped out this rubber ink stamp and put a red armadillo on the back of each hand. It was just weird," I say.

"Not if you're a bouncer. Did he say anything?" AJ asks.

"He said, 'Welcome aboard. Armadillos are my favorite

animal. They're so misunderstood.' As if that explained everything."

"I don't know about the hand-stamp thing, but he once threw an AP style manual at the back of my head for not getting to the phone by the third ring," AJ says. "Then there was the time he came storming out of his office and swept everything off a reporter's desk. There were pens and note-books flying everywhere."

"What did the reporter do to piss him off?" I ask.

"Made a mistake on a big story. We had to print a re-traction. Harry was like a polar bear on crack. He kept screaming, 'Sloppy desk, sloppy reporting,' over and over again. I seriously thought his head was going to spin around and we'd have to call in a priest for an exorcism."

I sneak a glance at Harry, who's happily playing basket-ball with Dan, one of the pressmen. Harry just seems like a fortysomething overgrown kid to me. AJ is not the type to exaggerate, though. With his nearly shoulder-length brown hair, ripped-knee jeans, and seemingly endless collection of classic-rock tees, AJ is the embodiment of laid-back. He's starting his second year at Rutgers-Newark this fall, but I gather he's more interested in playing drums with his band, Love Gas, than in working for the *New York Times* someday. Sometimes I think he might seem a lot cuter if he just tried a little harder.

The phone rings. Maybe it's a funeral director with, like, seven or eight obits. That would be sweet. Then we can deep-six the pastry-chef feature.

"Obit desk," I answer.

"You sound so friendly when you say that. It's creepy, you know?"

Ugh. Shelby. Not sweet.

"Do not call me on this line. I told you that."

"But when I call your cell, I don't get to hear you say 'obit desk.' Besides, you've been screening me all day."

"I'm busy," I say.

"You're not still angry about the Rob McGinty thing, are you? Because I thought I was helping, really. You're always so afraid to talk to him, and I think you'd have a chance with Rob if you'd just—"

"Look, we'll talk later, okay?" I say through clenched teeth. Please, oh, please let her summer job at the mall come through.

"You're not going to let this ruin our last real summer, are you?"

"Not the last-real-summer thing again. I'm hanging up now."

"Don't you—"

Click.

"Was that your spacey friend again?" AJ asks.

Shelby's right about one thing, I've always been shy around most guys. Not AJ, though. On my first day, AJ and I did these mock interviews of each other as part of my training. The exercise lasted only an hour, but the Q&A between us never stopped.

"Yes, she calls the obit desk almost as much as your

girlfriend, Jessica," I say. "Call, text, do *something*. Communication is the key to any healthy relationship."

"She's not my girlfriend, she's my . . . I don't know," he says.

"I'm sure Jessica appreciates you referring to her as your I-don't-know."

AJ just shrugs. "Things are unclear at the moment."

"Right. I understand completely."

I don't, really. In fact, I've been trying to get a read on this situation since I started working here. AJ says this Jessica person is not his girlfriend, but he wears a black leather cord around his neck with a plain silver ring that looks, well, girlie. Is it Jessica's? Would a guy wear a girl's ring? Seems odd. When it comes to dating, though, what do I know? I'm more familiar with the surface of Mars (thanks to NASA's excellent website).

We stare at each other for a few seconds before I continue. "Anyway, if Shelby calls on the obit line again, can you do me a favor and pretend you're my boss and tell her you'll fire me if she doesn't stop calling?"

"No problemo," he says. "If you didn't sound twelve, you could probably do the same for me with Jessica."

"Shut up," I say. "Just be thankful no one can tell how short you are from the sound of your voice."

"Short? I'm not short. Five-nine is average. Like you should talk."

He's right. People who are five-one should not throw stones.

"Sorry. It's just that Shelby is making me insane. Her foreign-exchange-student boyfriend returned to his homeland, and she suddenly remembered she's the yin to my yang," I say.

"So, your friend turned into a total ho this year, and now you don't like her?"

"Nooo. I told you. The party? She blabbed to that guy and made it sound like I was totally crushing on him. Plus, she abandoned me all year long while she strolled the halls holding hands and making out with *Olaf*," I say.

"Bitter much?"

Maybe I am. A boyfriend—and perhaps some help in the boobage department—would make it so much easier to navigate the slim passageways between high school social circles. If Chestnutville High is as good as it gets, I'm going to pull a Sylvia Plath. Last real summer? I'm still waiting for my *first* real summer. My first real everything.

"Why don't you get started on that feature obit while I make a coffee run?" AJ says.

"Why don't *you* get started on the feature while *I* make the coffee run?"

"Because *I* can drive through Dunkin' Donuts, which is faster than walking to the deli. Plus, you're a way better writer," AJ says.

"Flattery will get you nowhere."

"Yes, but my car will get me to Dunkin' Donuts."

"Fine," I say, silently cursing the state of New Jersey for making the legal age to drive without an adult seventeen, and my guidance counselor for hooking me up with this summer job after my parents expressed their concern that working the Snack Shack at the community pool wasn't challenging enough. Honor Society and Advanced Placement classes just aren't enough for those two. It's not easy being the sole offspring of two lawyers. A little sibling diversion would have been nice. Still, I'm a people pleaser by nature.

So in April I went to Mr. Arbeeny for some advice about finding a summer job that would look good on my college applications. I told him I like to write—my straight-A grades in all my English classes prove I've got some skills in that area. So Mr. Arbeeny mentioned my "flair for writing"—how very guidance counselorish of him—to his old friend Harry, and here I am. At first I was excited to have a summer job doing real writing. I've harbored secret dreams of starting my own blog for a while now. But, somehow, I didn't anticipate I'd be fetching coffee for editors and writing about dead people all day.

On the upside, here's what I've discovered: High school, if you live long enough, doesn't mean all that much when you're dead. Obit writers don't get to say a lot about a life in four paragraphs. There just isn't space to mention GPAs or SAT scores, honor rolls or varsity letters, Chess Club or in-school suspension. But were my life to end right now, at best my own obit would be short, like me. At this point, all I've got is a decent headline.

I search for the funeral home's number so I can get the scoop on the pastry chef. I sigh and pick up the phone.

Oddly enough, even though I'm surrounded by death all day, this gig is tons easier than high school. I enjoy being the youngest person in the room. It's like I'm the foreign-exchange student around here.

"Moronica! Where's my feature?" Bernadette yells.

Except I'm not Olaf. I'm Moronica.

chapter two

Breaking News

It's finally Friday. A disturbing number of people have taken their last breath in the past twenty-four hours. For the past hour, AJ and I have been sitting at our face-to-face desks typing nonstop, with phone receivers wedged between our ears and shoulders. Name. Born. Died. Survivors. Services. Obits have a poetic structure all their own. My neck is stuck in this position. Headsets would be a nice addition to the obit desk.

"We are *so* not doing a feature obit," I hear AJ say as he slams down his phone. "I just took three in a row. That makes twenty-seven."

I'm about to hang up my own phone and fist-bump AJ when the back door slams open and in steps Michael Fishman, the cool, married thirtysomething who sits beside me. He angrily swats down the Nerf basketball as it arcs for the net, much to the dismay of the moaning copy-desk editor who launched it. Michael tosses his reporter's notebook onto his desk and puts his hands on his hips. He surveys the newsroom for a few seconds before taking a deep breath and sitting down.

"I just got called an a-hole by that a-hole," he says.

"Mayor troubles?" I ask.

"Mayor troubles."

The *Herald Tribune* has been trying to prove that the mayor of East Passaic, the town Michael covers, misused federal funding and gave his friends no-show city jobs. (They can't teach this stuff in social studies.) Harry refers to the mayor and his cronies as Robin Hoods. He amuses himself with his play on words.

"What happened?" I ask Michael.

"I questioned him about Sy Goldberg being on the payroll without there being much evidence to support that he actually *works* in exchange for the fat salary he's collecting. I've talked to a lot of folks and no one has ever seen this guy. So the mayor says, 'You're an a-hole. Sy Goldberg is dying. You're an a-hole to even ask that.'" Michael pauses and raises one eyebrow, a look that cracks me up before he even utters a word.

"And I said, 'Yes, but is he still on the payroll?' Am I right? I mean, it begs the question, how much work can a dying man do?"

Michael does not shy away from the tough questions. I love listening in on his phone interviews and anxiously await his caustic comments when he hangs up. I wish I were doing real reporting like Michael, but sadly, me and AJ are newsroom bottom-feeders. In addition to obits, we write web copy, compile blurbs for the Community Calendar and Arts Happenings sections, type up movie timetables, sort mail, answer phones, go on food and coffee runs, organize stacks of extra newspapers, and do whatever else Harry commands. AJ writes music and concert reviews too, but I haven't proven myself worthy of bigger stories yet.

"Well, *we* don't think you're an a-hole," I say.

"And more important, it's Friday," AJ says.

Michael sits down at his desk and begins to type. "I've just got to bang out this feature on the grand opening of the mayor's new coffee shop slash bookstore, and then I'm outta here."

"Screw the feature," AJ says. "I wouldn't do him any favors."

"Yeah, especially after what he called you," I add.

"It's part of the game. You try to make your sources happy. Even if he's a total bastard, I've got to keep him talking to me. Anyway, the favor is more for his daughter. He's opening the place for her." Michael turns to me. "In fact, it's in your town, Sam."

"A new coffee-shop and bookstore in Chestnutville?" I say. Hmm. It actually sounds like the kind of place I'd go.

"Yeah, his daughter lives there," Michael says. "Anyway, this won't take long, and then happy hour is starting early for me today."

I glance at the clock. It's only five. Cool. I should be out of here by six o'clock, myself. I'm gonna go for a run (I'm working up the nerve to run my first 10k at the end of September), take a bubble bath, and watch *Sixteen Candles* on DVD with my mom. We're in the middle of a 1980s film marathon.

My homebody fantasy is interrupted by the sudden blaring of the police scanner. I'm used to its omnipresent crackling in the newsroom and have come to regard it as a strange heartbeat. But at the moment, Rocco, the police reporter, is cranking up the volume. I fear the off-the-charts decibel count is causing me permanent hearing loss.

"What the hell?" AJ asks. He swivels his chair in Rocco's direction.

Sirens and horns from a fire truck, or two, or three, drown out the scanner's urgent cacophony.

"Four-alarm fire in Clifton," Rocco says. He's already in motion, grabbing notebooks and pens from his desk. "There's been an explosion."

"Call in as soon as you can so we can get something up on the website," Harry says as Rocco bolts for the door, nearly slamming into a chair and doing a complete three-sixty before recovering.

"Fishman! Are you on deadline?" Harry says.

"No." There goes Michael's happy hour.

"Follow Rocco to the fire. Intern scum!" Harry yells in our general direction. Coming from anyone else, it would sound offensive, but I caught on quickly to his brand of humor. "Plan on staying late and answering phones."

And there goes my five-mile run. I'm bummed. I need my weekly long runs to clear my head. It's also when I get my best ideas. I've been mulling over concepts for my blog, when and if I ever start one. I've thought about calling it Something to Blog About, but that's taken, or Notes from the High School Trenches, but that's too long.

Harry's booming voice interrupts my blog musings. He barks out more orders to others around the room. To the copy desk: "Bernie, what's our page one look like right now? Start making room." To reporters: "Meg, I may pull you to do local react if anyone dies." To the city desk editors: "Grace, as soon as Rocco calls in, tell him to start feeding you copy."

Everyone seems caught up in the heightened energy brought on by the fire. Except yours truly. I've been rendered temporarily immobile as people whirl around me like leaves on a windy day. I snap out of it when the air-raid siren sounds, calling volunteer fire departments from surrounding towns.

"That can't be good," I say. My stomach is in scary-movie mode.

AJ doesn't look up from his texting. Bandmate or Jessica the pseudogirlfriend, no doubt. I get an unexpected pang thinking it may be the latter but quickly shake it away. I need to calm my nervous energy, so I spend the next half hour putting a huge pile of press releases in date order.

When the city-desk phone finally rings, Grace Yad-
lowski, the assistant city-desk editor, snatches it up. Usually
the editors wait for me or AJ to answer. Answering phones
comes with our intern status. At least we get paid, which
technically makes us editorial assistants, but Harry says "intern scum" sounds punchier. He also doesn't believe anyone should work for free—even high school interns. Despite
his gruffness, Harry's fair. Underneath that polar-bear ex-
terior, Winnie the Pooh is alive and well.

"Rocco! What's going on?" Grace says.

Everyone in the newsroom is eavesdropping and holding their collective breath, waiting for Grace's reaction.

"A five-story apartment building collapsed," she yells.
"Three people confirmed dead. Unknown number trapped
inside." Grace turns toward her monitor and starts typing.

"Meg!" Harry yells. "Get down there and help Rocco
and Fishman." Harry turns toward the obit desk. "Sam,
AJ! If we get victims' names, I may need you two to start
calling around for reactions."

Harry uses the remote to flip through channels on the
overhead TV until he lands on a local news station with
fire footage. I'm at once horrified and excited. Adrenaline
pumps through my veins, raises my body temperature, and
makes my chest all splotchy—my usual nervous reaction.
It's very attractive.

"I'll be in the back," Harry tells Grace. I watch him
walk through the swinging doors on the far side of the
rectangular room. He's probably going to talk to the press

guys. We're one of the few newspapers left that *have* press guys, but that may all be ending soon. The paper has been losing money, and there's been talk about shutting the presses down and sending the paper out for printing. It would stink to end a century-long run, but it's better than having to close our doors completely.

Because the *Herald Tribune* still prints the paper on the premises, the newsroom is more like the front office of a warehouse than a corporate work environment. The ceiling is high, with exposed fluorescent lighting, like the kind in a school gym. The metal desks are clumped together in groups of four or five. There are no partitions of any kind, except for the ceilingless walls around Harry's office, the conference room, and sports.

"This bites," AJ says to no one in particular. "We're just waiting around."

He's right. Despite the amped-up newsroom chatter— due to both the TV and the police scanner being louder than usual—it's pretty much business as usual for everyone else. The last obit cleared the copy desk a while ago, and just when I'm thinking Harry is about to send us home, Rocco calls Grace with two names. There are still only three confirmed dead, but Rocco says firefighters from every surrounding town are struggling through the charred debris in a desperate search and rescue. The fire is just smoldering now.

Harry comes over to the obit desk with the victims' information. One was an elderly man who lived alone;

the other, a high school track star who went to Northside High School. He gives AJ the older man, Mitchell Dawson, and I get the teenager, Anton Richards.

"I don't know what you're gonna get right now on the old guy," Harry says to AJ. "Meg is working the scene for react too. D'Angelo, see if you can find the high school track coach, and start with him."

My first instinct is to Google the track team, but then I remember the stacks of local yearbooks dating back to the 1940s that we keep in our makeshift library behind the partition, where the sports department lives. I jump up from my seat and head off in that direction, but when I reach the door to sports, I realize an online search is probably faster. I reverse course, then spin around again, because I'd rather look through the yearbooks.

"What are you doing?" AJ asks. "You look like an indecisive squirrel trying to cross the street. Those are the ones that always wind up as roadkill, you know."

"Shut up. I'm just trying to find the coach's name."

"Sit down, Squirrel Girl with Limited Search Engine Knowledge," he says while looking at his computer screen. "I've got it right here. Let's see if he's listed."

"Uh, thanks. Any leads on your old man?"

"Nope. I'm trying to figure out if he has relatives in the area or belonged to any local groups," he says.

Lucky AJ. I'm dreading this phone call. At least the chill in my body made my red splotches fade fast. I wind up retrieving the Northside High School yearbook anyway.

Yes, I'm stalling. But I'm also curious to see what Anton Richards looks like. Looked like.

I begin paging through the yearbook, and I'm surprised by my own sense of longing as I see the happy faces of the kids in French Club, Student Council, and marching band. I flip to the pages with all the sports. In the Varsity Track section there's a close-up of Anton clearing a hurdle. A simple black-and-white pic, and yet I can feel his grace and speed. I turn the page to the team picture. A smiling Anton is kneeling in the front row. There will be an empty space there next spring. My mouth goes dry. Anton is now as still as these photographs. Was he burned badly? Did he die from smoke inhalation before he felt the flames? Will his parents be able to recognize him? My dark thoughts make me shiver.

I reach for my bottled water as I close the book. When I again feel capable of speech, I pick up the phone and dial. A woman answers.

"Hello. I'd like to speak with Coach Davis," I say. "This is Samantha D'Angelo from the *Herald Tribune*. I'm working on a story about the Paterson fire."

I hear muffled voices as the woman covers the mouthpiece. A man speaks next.

"This is Coach Davis," says a deep voice.

"I'm sorry to bother you, sir. I'm working on a story about the Paterson fire."

"Fire?" he asks.

"Yes, sir. A five-story apartment building collapsed, and . . ." I trail off.

How am I supposed to tell this guy that one of the kids he coaches is dead? I don't have much experience with this. I'm only sixteen. I don't know many dead people. Books and TV hospital dramas are my sole sources in this area.

"Young lady, are you there?"

"Oh, yes, I'm sorry. It's just that I don't know how to say this, but we've learned, it seems, one of the guys on your track team didn't make it out of the fire."

"What? Who?" he asks.

"Anton Richards."

There's a moment of silence on the other end. "Are you sure? Maybe it's a different Anton Richards," he says.

"My editor told me that this Anton ran track for Northside," I say.

"Oh my God! No. My God," Coach Davis says, his voice breaking.

"Sir?" I say quietly, not knowing which I fear more, pressing this poor, shocked man for a quote or telling Harry I just came up empty-handed. My heart thumps loud and fast in my ears.

And then the line goes dead.

"I guess he can't talk right now," I say. I put both hands on my forehead and then rub my eyes. I screwed it up. My first chance to do something real, and I screwed it up.

AJ looks at me sympathetically. "You want me to call him back in an hour?" he offers.

"Nah, that's okay," I say. "I'll do it."

My eyes are welling up both from my fear of Harry and disappointment in myself. My heart is breaking for Anton and his family. Someone my age just died. It feels so wrong. There will be no first day of school for him this year. No more track medals. No graduation tassel hanging from the rear-view mirror. Obits are supposed to be for dead old people.

With the back of my hand, I swish away the tears threatening to escape my eyes before AJ notices. Then I go over to the city desk and tell Harry about the coach. Harry grimaces and gives me a sharp "okay." I feel my neck turning red and retreat to my desk, where I torture myself for the next fifteen minutes. I'm considering looking through the yearbook for the names of Anton's teammates when Harry cuts us a break and tells us we can go home. It's like a trig test I forgot to study for just got postponed.

"Good job, you two," he says. "Meg and Fishman are on the way back. They can take it from here."

"Harry," I say. "I'm sorry about the coach, I—"

"It's all right, D'Angelo. We got it."

I'm pretty sure he's not mad. Or maybe I'm just being overly optimistic. AJ appears beyond unaffected by the evening's drama. I don't know how he does it. Without thinking, I start typing on a blank screen.

Anthony John Bartello, drummer for the local band Love Gas, died Friday. He was 19. A student at Rutgers University's Newark campus, AJ, as he was known to his friends and bandmates, finally succumbed to the pressures of trying so hard not to care.

"You want a ride home?" AJ asks. "I'm on my way to band practice. I can drop you off."

Select all. Delete.

"Huh? Oh, sure. Thanks," I say. "I'll call my parents and let them know they can put their jammies on."

———

As we get into AJ's Jeep Cherokee, my phone vibrates. It's Shelby. I'm tired and don't feel much like talking to her, but I answer.

"What?" I say softly.

"Don't say no," she says.

"You haven't asked me anything."

"Wanna go to a party at Ryan Mauriello's tonight?"

"The football crowd? What are you trying to do to me?"

"Oh, come on. Even if Rob's there, he's not going to bring up what I said. Everyone was pretty lit that night."

"Forget it," I say, and hit end call. I switch my phone back to the ring setting (it needs to be on vibrate in the newsroom), only to hear it play "Don't Talk to Strangers" less than thirty seconds later. I listen to the entire chorus before I answer.

"Rick Springfield? Could you have picked a *less* cool ringtone?" AJ asks.

"What?" I say, to both AJ and Shelby, who I know is on the other end. "My dad plays bass in an eighties cover band."

"I know," says confused Shelby.

AJ just nods. Shelby keeps going.

"Okay, Sam. How about this? If you're not having fun after, like, half an hour, we can leave. Please. I promise."

I'm about to hang up on her again, but then I picture Anton. And the way he was smiling in that team picture. Yesterday at this time, he was still here. He should be on his way to a party tonight with his best friend.

"Fifteen minutes," I say.

Shelby pauses, slightly stunned. "Okay, fifteen minutes."

"Deal," I say. "I'll go to the dumb party." I surprise myself *and* AJ, who raises both eyebrows at me when I glance toward him. He has watched from the front row as I've avoided Shelby. But this isn't about her, it's about me. And Anton Richards. Tonight, I just want to be an ordinary teenager while I've still got the chance. It's probably time to let Shelby off the hook. Anyway, who else do I have to hang out with? The other girls in our group are away this summer. Caitlin has a beach house, and Ashley went to California to stay with her dad.

"Cool. My mom can drive. We'll pick you up in an hour. Oh, and Sam?"

"What?"

"Uh, never mind. See you soon."

But if I know Shelby, and I do, she was going to tell me to wear makeup.

chapter three

Weekend Entertainment

At home, my mom all too quickly gives me permission to go to the party. I watch her pour veggies into a bowl and open the dip we were going to share. Maybe I'll cancel on Shelby. Mom intuits my mood shift. She looks up at me and smiles.

"We'll see *Sixteen Candles* some other time," she says. "We can have a John Hughes film festival."

Why am I getting flashbacks of her coaxing me through the door of Pixie Preschool? Even without makeup, her almond-shaped brown eyes look extra bright. Perhaps she's glowing from within at the thought of me getting out and not sitting in front of the TV with her watching classic teen movies.

That's the strange dichotomy of me. I love to watch idealized versions of kids my age, and yet, I don't know how to live among them. It's not high school I have the problem with; it's me in high school. I'm like the ugly step-sister trying to jam her big nasty foot into that delicate glass slipper.

"Keep your phone on, sweetie." She licks some dip off her finger and then twists her gorgeous auburn curls into a loose bun, just like I'm in the habit of doing. It looks better on her. "And call or text me if you're going to be superlate."

"I will," I say. My mom and I are in touch constantly, something that might bug other girls my age, but I've always been fine with it.

———

At ten thirty, Shelby's mom honks out front. With a September birthday, Shelby's behind me in the driver's license department. In all other areas, she's eons ahead.

"Wake me when you get in so I know you got home," Mom says as I kiss her cheek.

"And try to have *fun*," Grandma yells from her plush blue recliner in front of the TV.

She's watching the news. Like most older people, she's obsessed with the weather, but she loves those cable talk shows too. Raging liberals, conservative stalwarts—it doesn't matter to her. She watches them all and has a pretty open mind for a gal her age.

"Okay, Gram!" I reply, heading for the front door.

"She's right. Enjoy yourself," Mom says. Almost pleads. My mom is happy Shelby gets me out of the house.

Shelby's mom is happy I keep Shelby from joining a cult or getting arrested. It's an arrangement that has been working since Shelby and I both took the wrong bus home on the first day of kindergarten. Our frantic moms, who discovered that they both had five-year-old daughters and no other children, bonded that afternoon, and so did we. Back then, our families had a lot in common. It stayed that way until Shelby's dad left when we were in third grade. She cried all the time that year, not about him exactly, just in general. I remember I used to carry extra tissues in my backpack, just for her. I've never shaken the feeling that, somehow, I'm responsible for Shelby.

I'm quiet on the drive over to the party. My palms are sweaty. Is it too late to bail? When we arrive at Ryan's house, Shelby shouts at her mom to keep driving and makes her drop us around the corner.

Shelby's mom frowns as she pulls up to the curb. "Embarrassed to be seen with me, huh?" she says.

"Oh, Ma. Don't be so sensitive. You remember what it was like," Shelby says as she puts a hand on her mom's shoulder and kisses her cheek. "Meet you here later?"

"Better watch out. Maybe I'll pull up in the driveway and honk the horn," Shelby's mom says with a laugh.

"Thank you, Diane," I say. I've called Shelby's mom by her first name for as long as I can remember.

"Why, you're very welcome, Sam," Diane says. Her hint isn't lost on Shelby.

"*Thanks*, Ma. Sheesh."

We walk around the corner and follow the music and noise emanating from Ryan Mauriello's backyard. I bite my lower lip, no doubt removing any trace of cinnamon gloss. "I can't believe I let you talk me into this party," I say to Shelby as we walk through the gate.

"You know me. I can talk you into anything. Like that afterparty at Ike's? The deejay? You thought we'd get in trouble, but it was awesome."

"We *did* get in trouble."

"Oh, that's right, we did. Drew was cute, though, right?"

Shelby took off with Ike and left me talking to this guy named Drew all night.

"He was, like, seven feet tall and had on a black T-shirt with skeletons in various sexual positions."

"I don't remember the T-shirt," Shelby says.

"You don't remember much."

"You had a great time. Admit it."

It's true, I did, but I say nothing. Still, my face gives me away.

"See?" Shelby says, pointing to my suppressed smile. "Your life's more interesting with me around."

Even though Shelby leads me over to the dark side sometimes, part of me does enjoy it. Her confidence is contagious, and her laugh is infectious. When I'm with her, I forget my uptight Sam ways and tap into my inner Shelby. And most times, I manage to keep us both out of trouble.

As we walk toward the patio, I'm like a black-and-white sketch stepping into a living, full-color Abercrombie & Fitch catalog. The girls are poised around the in-ground pool in bikini tops and sarongs, and there's no shortage of bare-chested guys with six-packs I thought possible only in infomercials. I don't know what I fear more about parties, having people look at me or not being noticed at all.

"I guess I missed the Evite regarding the island theme," I say.

Shelby frowns at my maroon Decemberists T-shirt, denim miniskirt, and flip-flops.

"What?" I say. "I wore makeup." Why am I here? It was all that fire excitement. Damned endorphins—great for a jump start, short on follow-through.

I scan the crowd for signs of Rob McGinty and his girlfriend, Liza. Rob has black hair and icy blue eyes, and I've been in love with him since the sixth grade, when he kissed me during spin the bottle. It wasn't a *kiss* kiss. But still. It meant something. To me at least. When we were young, I thought he liked me, too. We used to walk to school together.

But then junior high happened, and whatever I had going on in sixth grade, puberty stole from me. Add braces and a constellation of pimples to the glasses I already wore, and I became an easy target for insults. Shelby says I've always been too sensitive. Even back then, when she was nerdier, Shelby never cared what kids said about her. I tried talking to Rob sometimes, but once, some kids passing by in the hall started barking. I didn't talk to him at all after that. I was too humiliated. And maybe I expected him to stand up for me. Shelby always did. Still does.

Maybe I'm no longer that awkward seventh-grade girl,

but my own metamorphosis from ugly ducking to swan stalled out in the Cornish-game-hen stage. At some point, I decided self-imposed exile was safer than putting myself out there.

"Relax. I bet Rob won't even be here," Shelby says, and gives my hand a squeeze.

"I hope you're right."

"Let's get a beer," she says.

"You know I don't drink."

"Maybe you should start. It helps when you're shy," Shelby says matter-of-factly. "Drinking and showing cleavage. Remember that for the next party."

"I don't *have* cleavage."

"Two words: Cleavage Cupcakes."

With honey blond hair and a chest that enters a room a full two seconds before she does, Shelby always gets noticed. Me? I'm more cute than pretty. Despite my pure Mediterranean bloodline, I'm not blessed with olive skin or thick hair like everyone else in my family and most people in my town. I'm not saying I *want* to be overly tan and flaunt an Italian-princess necklace, but it would make things easier. I'm, like, a pasty white, wispy-haired exile in Guidoville. My brown eyes are just that—brown—which may be interesting to the guy who wrote "Brown-Eyed Girl" but isn't, really, to anyone else. So I don't think putting gel inserts into my bra is going to help.

Reluctantly, I follow Shelby as she shimmies her way through the crowd toward the keg, smiling and saying hello to people like she's walking the red carpet. Year after year, I keep hoping the Shelby-tude will rub off on me—a silent wish that for better or worse tethers us together. I hold my breath, hoping it will render me invisible.

"Shelby!" yells a guy standing by the keg filling red plastic cups.

"Hey, Mark," Shelby answers.

"You look great!" Mark says.

"Thanks," Shelby says. She puts a hand on my shoulder. "This is my friend—"

But Mark cuts her off, either because he doesn't hear or doesn't care. "So Olaf went back to Germany, huh?" he says as he hands Shelby a foamy beer, which she passes to me.

"Yeah, he's been gone for two weeks. Can I have another one of those?" Shelby asks, pointing to the keg.

"Huh? Oh, yeah," Mark says. He fills another cup for Shelby.

It's as if I'm not even here. *Careful what you wish for.*

"So . . . are you two doing the long-distance thing?" Mark asks.

Shelby shakes her head. "We broke up before he left."

Mark, who doesn't bother to conceal that this is good news as far as he's concerned, grins big as he pours himself a beer.

"Hey, come with me," Mark says. "You gotta check out the hot tub."

As he pulls Shelby toward the pool area, she glances

over her shoulder with a smile, like she can't help being dragged away.

"Sam, come with us," she says.

"I'll wait here for you," I call after her.

"Sure?"

"I'm sure."

I smell my beer and take a tentative sip. Yuck. The taste hasn't grown on me, but at least I can carry my cup around and make it look like I'm drinking. For a few more seconds, I stand where Shelby left me, not sure where to look or who to talk to. It's like being left alone in an unfamiliar subway station as the train pulls away. Time to look for the bathroom. I'll reapply my lip gloss and buy some time before I look for Shelby.

Keeping my head down, I squish through the crowd and try to get beyond the herd as fast as possible. I make it to the concrete patio, where some guys are taking turns drinking beer through a funnel while cheering each other on. I don't get drinking games. I don't get drinking. Maybe because I don't like beer. Wine has always been offered freely at my house, and even though I like it, getting drunk isn't an option. It would trigger two of my biggest fears: puking and losing control.

I step through the patio door and into the kitchen, which smells like a mixture of beer, sweat, and various colognes. A group of guys and girls are gathered around the granite breakfast bar playing Quarters with what appear to be different types of hard alcohol.

"Hey, girl!" shouts one of the guys. I've seen him with Rob. Josh something.

I shift my eyes left and right, trying to figure out if he's talking to me.

"Yeah, you. Cute girl in the reddish shirt. Don't look so angry," he says. "Come play with us."

So this is my life story. A decent-enough-looking guy starts off calling me cute and then, because I don't exude the appropriate amount of excitement (I have *no* idea how to flirt—I fully admit this), it quickly turns bad and I become Angry Girl. Angry? Do I look angry? People are always doing that to me—telling me to smile, asking me what's wrong, when I'm perfectly content. I just have a pouty-shaped mouth, that's all.

"Uh, I'm just looking for the bathroom," I say. "Maybe later."

I even smile with some teeth.

"Whatever. Be that way," he says.

Another gift. I'm always pissing people off without trying. Typical me. I walk down the hall and into the foyer, looking for a bathroom. When I find the half bath near the front door, the stench of vomit is so strong, I almost get sick myself. I decide to try upstairs. Maybe there's a bathroom in the master bedroom.

When I arrive on the upstairs landing, all the bedroom doors are closed. I open the first one, and I'm greeted by the site of a bare ass on top of a seminude girl. I quickly snap the door shut as someone says, "Who the hell was that?" Quickly, I abort my bathroom search and dash down the stairs and out the front door. It's not like I really had to go, anyway.

I circle back into the yard again. Should I bother to look for Shelby or just find some space where I can avoid butts in the buff and angry Quarters players? As I wander through the crowd, I'm trying so hard to avoid making eye contact—or any other kind of contact, for that matter—that I don't see the rather large guy, who must be a linebacker, stumbling toward me. He slams into my side and launches me into another guy, who, when he turns around, I recognize as Rob McGinty. He looks angry for a split second, then tilts his head and gives me an odd half smile.

"I'm sorry," I mumble. "I was pushed."

I'm about to break free when Rob grabs my elbow. "Sam D'Angelo? Are you okay? You don't look so good." Super. Just the words I want to hear from our star quarterback *and* class president. The cliché of being Rob borders on ridiculous.

"I'm fine," I say. "It must be the beer."

Rob grins. "A lightweight, huh?"

"Are you kidding? This is my fourth cup."

Rob puts up his hands up in surrender. "I stand corrected. I'm surprised. You don't seem the type."

How would Rob know what type I am? For the rest of us, high school is like a sadistic game of musical chairs where everyone competes for a few chances at fitting in. When the music stops, most of us are left standing. But

Rob, he doesn't even have to play the game. And yet he's nice, which somehow makes it worse. A girl like me could never date a guy like him—things like that only happen in movies, where the plain girl is actually some gorgeous actress without makeup. About an hour and fifteen minutes into the film, the girl buys a new outfit and applies some mascara, and suddenly the prom king is doinking himself in the head for not realizing sooner how hot she is.

"I saw your name in the newspaper," Rob says out of nowhere.

This gets my attention. "You read the obit page?"

Forget the obit page. I'm just shocked someone our age reads the newspaper.

"My mom spotted it. That's pretty cool, though. You were always good at writing."

Wow. Rob noticed my name and remembers I like writing. His compliment is just sinking in when Rob's girlfriend, Liza, and her friends arrive. Men aren't dogs, girls are. That's why they travel in packs. Liza wraps her arm around one of Rob's biceps. My stomach twists.

"Who's your friend?" she asks, looking me up and down.

"Uh, this is Sam D'Angelo," Rob says.

"Oh, *right*," she says, and giggles, making it clear she knows what Shelby said to Rob at the last party.

Is fuchsia lipstick toxic? I hope so.

Not wanting to stick around and cause any trouble, I offer an explanation as to why I'm talking to her boyfriend and plan my escape. "Someone pushed me into Rob," I explain. "Sorry!"

"S'okay," Rob says.

He looks like he wants to say something more, but I don't give him a chance. After a quick wave and an apologetic smile, I make a beeline for an open space in the yard. I scan for a location near the fence, where I can observe without additional human interaction. My skin is hot with the embarrassment of bumping into Rob, literally, and having his girlfriend laugh at me.

I admit it, I'm jealous of girls like Liza who always have boyfriends. She and Rob have been together since freshman year, and it seems like no one goes out of their way to insult couples. It's like they're living in some U.N.-sanctioned territory—the shaded area of a Venn diagram, where all the circles overlap.

I find an empty lawn chair and wait for Shelby to finish doing whatever with Mark, her latest Y chromosome. I'm far enough away from the crowd and music to hear the chirping crickets and cicadas in the trees behind me. I wonder; do all bugs get to sing? Or is it only the best and most beautiful who hit the suburban sound waves on summer nights? Is there a bug version of me out there, longing to be the lead singer but always ending up in the chorus or, worse yet, silent and unable to find her voice?

I take out my phone so I look busy. I tab to the *Herald Tribune*'s website. It's not the best, but at least we have one. I think about Rob noticing my byline on the obit page, and my mood lifts. I fantasize about helping Michael prove his mayor's up to no good. My name could end up on the front page. What if I scored an interview with the elusive Sy Goldberg? It wouldn't make me a shoe-in for prom queen, but it would be something, wouldn't it? Perhaps the quiet recognition of a byline suits me.

An hour later, when my phone's entertainment abilities are waning, I spot Shelby. She stumbles across the backyard, her serpentine path moving in my general direction. When she finally reaches me, she puts two hands on one hip and tries to steady herself.

"There you are! I've been looking for you."

Not that hard, apparently.

"Is your shirt on inside out?" I ask, frowning. It is.

"No!" she says, looking down to make sure, but upsetting her equilibrium in the process. She starts to sway.

"Let's go," I say. "I'm done." I begin to pry myself loose from the plastic lawn chair. My bare legs are stuck from sitting so long. Great. Now I'll have to walk out of here with a waffle pattern on my thighs.

"Sam, you aren't mad at me, are you?" she slurs. I sit back down.

"No," I say. I'm really not mad at Shelby. It's not her fault I don't have fun at these things. But I *am* worried about her drinking and what she does once she's trashed. She turns into a different person, not the Shelby I know. I don't want her getting a reputation. She's better than that.

"Good, because you're my best friend. And I'm so, so

sorry I blabbed to Rob. You know I love you. And you deserve a guy like him. Uh, and . . . Uh-oh, I'm gonna—"

I don't wait for her to finish her sentence. I rip myself out of the chair like a Band-Aid and move clear of Shelby's open mouth just in time to watch her projectile vomit splatter the chair where I was just sitting.

"Very nice," I say. "You're right. Maybe I should start drinking."

Shelby slumps down to her knees and starts to cry. Not good. Shelby always starts out crying about one thing and ends up crying about her father. It's one of the reasons I can never stay angry with her for long. I reach into the small purse I brought with me.

"Here," I say. "Have some gum. I'll call your mom." Without saying a word, I hand Shelby a tissue.

I am so over all things high school. I can't wait to get back to work.

chapter four

Book Review

wake up early Saturday morning thinking of Sy Goldberg. *Maybe I can help Michael find the evidence he needs to prove
the mayor has been up to no good,* I think as I tie the laces of my
running shoes and head downstairs to the garage, where the
treadmill lives. The house is still quiet.

I pop in my earbuds, step on the belt, and adjust the
speed. I know if I'm serious about doing a 10k this fall, I've
got to start training outside. Next time, I promise myself.
This is good enough for now. Treadmills and iPhones were
made for people like me. Running while hiding. It's a sport;
it's a way of life. I like the solitude of the garage. When I
run, I pretend I'm a different kind of girl. My best ideas
and fantasies come to me as I watch the red blip that is
me doing laps on my NordicTrack's screen.

*Mile One: I'm fronting a band. I'm the kind of female
rocker who can stand on a stage, uninhibited, and belt out a*

song. Oh, and I can play guitar too. Today at least. Some-
times it's drums.

Mile Two: A photographer snaps my picture as I receive
a New Jersey Press Association Award. I'm the youngest
reporter ever to be honored for her investigative journalism,
for my work on the Sy Goldberg story.

Mile Three: Rob McGinty leans on his car outside my
house, waiting to drive me to school. He's holding my vanilla
latte like he has every morning since he dumped Liza and
started dating me, the award-winning journalist.

I'm a sucker for a movie montage. I like mine with
power pop and alt-rock in my ears. Today, some harder
rock in the form of Love Gas made the playlist. AJ downloaded his band's songs for me. They're really good. I'm
glad. It would have been awkward to pretend I liked them.

By the time I finish my cooldown, I'm convinced I can
help Michael with his corrupt-mayor investigation, and I
have an idea about where to start. Without stopping to
think, I text AJ.

Wanna go to the mayor's coffee shop with me today?

That may be the first time I've asked a guy to do anything. But this is AJ. No reason to feel weird about it.

When I emerge from the steamy garage, Gram is at the
kitchen table doing a crossword puzzle.

"Morning, hon," she says when she sees me. "Coffee?"

"Thanks, Gram. I'm going to shower first. Where's Mom and Dad?"

"Your mother had to go into the office for a couple of hours," Gram says. "And your dad just went outside to cut the lawn."

"Got it," I say, then take a paper towel and wipe the sweat from my eyes. "I'm going to get cleaned up."

"Okay. I'll make a fresh pot when you're done."

"Sounds great. Thanks, Gram."

I check my phone on the way upstairs. No reply from AJ yet. It's not even nine. He's probably still sleeping. I should have waited.

After my shower, the hours tick by and I grow tired of obsessively checking my phone every three minutes for a return text. At noon, I call AJ. But when I dial, it goes straight to voice mail. That's when I decide I've got to do something, anything, besides stare at my phone. I find my dad and ask him to take me out for driving practice. Thirty minutes into our session, it's obvious this is a big mistake. On a good day, it's impossible for me to parallel park Dad's minivan, but today, I'm extra preoccupied. Did AJ think I was asking him out? Is he screening me? Is he with Jessica? Somewhere around one o'clock, my exasperated dad decides it's time to practice on the highway.

"Let's fill up the tank first," Dad says. "Pull into that station on the right."

"Okay."

I maneuver into Pit Stop behind a blue BMW with a

vanity plate that reads SHEDVL, which is either Yiddish or an ill-conceived abbreviation. In the driver's seat is a girl a little older than me who's feverishly plucking her eyebrows in the rearview mirror. The gas station attendants are half checking her out, half amused. Oddly enough, I'm inspired. If this girl remains undaunted by the attention her public grooming is attracting, surely I can *run* outside. There's nothing remotely odd or unexpected about that.

"Sam?" My dad's voice tears my focus away from the hypnotic plucking.

"What?"

"We can go now. The guy just gave me my credit card back," he said. "You're going to have to back up a little to get around this car. Be careful."

"Don't worry, I won't hit the plucker."

"What?"

"Nothing," I say. I turn around to make sure no one is coming into the gas station behind me and put the car in reverse.

Five minutes later, I'm headed down the on-ramp for the Garden State Parkway. Ugh. Merging. No one ever wants to let you in. After some wincing and teeth sucking from my dad, I finally navigate my way into the slow lane. I reach to turn on the radio, but my dad takes my right hand and puts it back at two o'clock.

"You drive," he says. "I'll deejay."

"Okay, but try to find a song that came out in the last three years. I'm not listening to 'Tom Sawyer' while you play air drums."

"Come on, Rush is timeless."

"If by timeless you mean old, then I agree."

"Just drive," he says.

"I'm driving," I say. "I'd rather be sitting in your seat playing with the radio, though."

"Sam, you live in New Jersey. You've got to learn to drive on highways. It's a matter of survival."

To me, the parkway is like high school. I'll put up with both if they take me someplace better. In the meantime, I keep a really safe distance. I don't want to get too close and get hurt.

My phone rings as I'm pulling onto our block. My dad gives me a look that says, *Don't even think about it,* and answers before I can stop him. He thinks he's being funny.

"Sam's phone. Who's calling? AJ?"

My heart does a double pump when I hear it's him. I'm not sure if I'm happy or relieved.

"Hold on. I'll turn the phone over to her in a sec. She's just pulling into the driveway. . . . No problem."

When the ignition is off, Dad hands me my phone and gets out of the car.

"Not bad. You're getting there," Dad says. "We'll take Mom's car next time."

"Thanks, Dad," I say, and then talk into my phone. "Hello?"

"Hey," AJ says. "I just got your text. Sorry about that. My phone's been off."

"Oh, yeah, sorry. It was early. I should've waited."

He doesn't mention the missed call from me, and I'm

48

relieved. I don't want him thinking I was desperate to get in touch with him.

After a long, awkward pause, AJ says, "So . . . still want to go?"

"To the coffee shop?"

"No. The Statue of Liberty."

"Ha, ha," I say, but I'm relieved to be back in banter mode with AJ. "I know it's probably a lame thing to do on a Saturday. But Michael mentioned it, and I was thinking—"

"The lameness can be overlooked."

"Cool."

"But it's got to be later—like, seven? I'm in the middle of a thing."

What kind of thing? A Jessica thing? Did I interrupt a date? It's getting hot in this car. I've got to step outside.

"Oh, yeah. Seven. That works," I say as I swing the door open.

"I'll come by your house?"

"Sure. Great." I'll be here doing nothing, because I don't have "a thing."

"Later," AJ says, and then he hangs up.

That night at the mayor's coffee shop/used bookstore, Bargain Books & Beans—how clever—I flip through well-worn copies of *Waiting for Godot* and one of my top-ten favorites, *Jane Eyre*. I've never read *Godot*, but the books were side by side on the shelf, and something about that intrigued me. AJ sits across from me. He's sporting a Beastie Boys T-shirt and reading the inside jacket of Slash's autobiography.

"Oh," I say, looking up from *Godot*. "I almost forgot. I checked out those Love Gas tunes today. Awesome."

"Yeah?" says AJ with a smile. "I mean, I *know* we're good. Just surprised you like us."

"Why? Because girls can't like harder music?"

"The Rick Springfield ringtone?"

He's got me there. I take out my phone and hand it to him.

"Do with this what you will."

"Any song?" AJ immediately tabs to my phone's settings.

"Your choice."

"Nice."

I decide it's time to get down to business. I lower my voice. "So. Do you think this place is legit or some kind of cover?"

AJ only half listens as he focuses on his music download. "Whataya mean?"

"I mean . . . do you think the mayor is up to something? Why would he open this place for his daughter?"

"Because she needs a job?" AJ looks at me now, raising his eyebrows as he takes a sip of his iced coffee.

"I guess."

"Is that why you wanted to come here?" AJ asks. A look I can't quite define passes over his face. "Research?"

The hot, red splotches are creeping up my chest toward my neck. I know it. "Sort of. I told you it was lame. I shouldn't have bothered you. Especially since you had a thing and all."

"No. It's all right. I just . . ." AJ shakes his head as if to clear away some train of thought. "The thing. It was for my mom."

I feel silly now for assuming he was with Jessica. "Oh, is it her birthday?"

"More like an anniversary," he says. "She died five years ago. We had a mass for her this morning. My grand-parents and uncle came. Then we all went to the cemetery and out to lunch."

"AJ, I'm so sorry." Without thinking, I reach over and pat his upper arm. "I didn't know."

"It's okay. I don't talk about her much. I probably should, right?"

I don't know what to say. So, for a few seconds, I say nothing. Finally, AJ scoops up his book and stands. "Ready to go? The smell of old books and coffee is getting to me."

I try to lighten the mood. "What did you expect? It's a coffee shop and they sell used books."

AJ shrugs and looks around. "Something more."

I try to gauge AJ's meaning as I look around the place myself. I'm not quite sure what I was expecting to find here. Granted, the place is still new, but there isn't much of a scene—no kids with laptops listening to music and drinking five-dollar lattes. No couples sharing dessert.

I'm feeling guilty for dragging AJ with me, so I take his book from him. "Here. It's on me," I say, and then walk toward the checkout. I place all three books on the counter—*Slash*, *Godot*, and *Jane*, what a combination.

We stand there for a few minutes in silence. AJ stares out the window. "This is a nice downtown you got here. Quaint."

Quaint. The word sounds funny coming from AJ. "After we pay, we can walk around. I'll give you the tour." And then I quickly add, "Only if you want. We don't have to." I don't want to pressure AJ into spending more lame time with me.

"A walking tour of Chestnutville? Let's do it."

"I can show you where Annie Oakley lived."

"Seriously? Well, now I can hardly wait to get started. If we ever get out of here, that is. Did the barista just up and leave for the night?" AJ asks.

"I was beginning to wonder the same thing." I look around to see if there's a bell or buzzer to ring for service. That's when I spot, behind the counter and next to a framed five-dollar bill, the health department certificate. My father's cousin, Dana, is an inspector for the town. She has told us one too many stories involving animal droppings and substandard refrigeration. So now I have this compulsion to check the health ratings of every restaurant I go into. I lean over the counter and strain my eyes to see what kind of rating this place received, but I still can't see. There's no sign of the barista, so I step behind the counter for a better look.

"What are you doing?" AJ asks.

"Shhh," I say as I lean close to the certificate.

The rating is "good"—that's a relief—and then I notice the names of the proprietors.

"No way!" I say, louder than I expected. *Giovanni Amato*—that's Michael's ne'er-do-well mayor—*and Sy Goldberg!*

chapter five

Death Notices

Monday morning. My dad drops me off early, before my scheduled shift, so I can do some research. I'm also anxious to see Michael and talk more about Bargain Books & Beans and Sy Goldberg. AJ and I phoned Michael on Saturday to tell him what we found out, but he's waiting until today to confront the mayor about his interesting choice for a business partner.

When I arrived at eight thirty this morning, only Harry, Alice (Harry's secretary), and Bernadette were here. No one gets in before the triumvirate. Since then, I've been perusing the *Herald Tribune*'s electronic archives for back stories about Michael's mayor. If I'm understanding it correctly, the city got a million-dollar federal grant to help low-income families reduce their energy bills by making their homes more energy efficient. The mayor hired Sy for $75,000 a year to oversee both the program and two additional employees. Interesting.

Is Sy short for something? Is that an actual first name? I wonder. First I Google "Sy Goldberg" and get some hits, then I simply type in "What is Sy short for?" Sylvan, Sylvester, Syahid? I check a few baby-name websites. Turns out, it could be any of those or just Sy or a bunch of other choices. I'm about to check the online white pages for Sy Goldberg when the phone rings—*again.*

If only my research didn't keep getting interrupted with obits and other death-related inquiries. I find I'm always explaining to some caller that death notices and in memoriams are paid services, that they're handled by the classified department and people can write whatever they want in those but there is a per word charge. At the *Herald Tribune,* the obits called in by funeral homes are free. (It's probably why our paper gets so many.) If only I were free of obit writing. It's not without its perks, however. For starters, it really helps put things like a stupid high school party in perspective. It's not even ten o'clock, and already there are three people I'm happy not to be: Helen Scavone, seventy-seven, retired teacher; Ernest Jacobs, ninety-one, optometrist; and Ina Mukin, ninety-two, housewife. All dead.

There's something to be said for breathing.

"Hey, Sam," Michael says.

I jump when I hear his voice behind me. "What are you doing here so early?"

Harry likes to see empty desks until deadline. He wants reporters out covering their towns, not sitting around the newsroom.

"I had to pick up something on my way to city hall. Wanna come with?"

"Really? I can? Now?"

"Sure, why not? Maybe I'll let you ask the mayor about his very silent business partner in the coffee biz. He can't call you an a-hole."

"Okay! Wait right here. Let me ask Bernie."

I bounce over to the copy desk, buoyed by the possibility of getting out of the newsroom to tag along with Michael. But Bernie quickly shoots me down. I should have known.

"Is AJ here?" She asks without looking up from her paper.

"Not yet."

"Then no."

"He'll be here any minute."

"Sorry. Back to the obit desk, Moronica. It's where all good writers start, and it's where they all end up."

I get the feeling Bernie invented snarky. I give her a cheesy smile and walk over to the door, where Michael is waiting.

"Can't go," I say.

Michael swings his leather messenger bag over his shoulder and picks up his keys.

"Bummer. Next time." Michael heads for the door, then turns around. "Good work, Sam. You've got some skills."

"Thank you!" His compliment eases my disappointment.

I sit down at the obit desk and type on a blank screen.

Bernadette Dunne, copy editor for the *Herald Tribune* since the days when the news was delivered by the Pony Express, died Monday. She was very, very old. Known to everyone except *Herald Tribune* intern Samantha D'Angelo as "Bernie," she died shortly after allowing the aforementioned D'Angelo to spend the morning away from the obit desk. Apparently, it could kill to be a little nicer.

Select all. Delete.

After Michael leaves, the newsroom is quiet except for Alice's squeaky chair and the intermittent crackling of the police scanner. The *Herald Tribune* has its own rhythm, and I like feeling the day gain momentum. The door behind me swings open with a bang, and I don't even have to look up to know who it is. The order is always the same.

First in, features editor Jack Ballard. Ext. 3214. Coffee, light and sweet.

It's funny. At school, I'm terrible with names. I struggle to make the most basic connection with kids my age.

"Morning, Jack."

"Hey there, Sam. You here already?"

He's a big teddy bear of a man who drives a Smart car that just seems to hug him. I've been collecting some feature ideas to pitch to Jack. AJ says as long as it doesn't interfere with our intern duties, Harry's usually cool with it.

Thunk. The back door again. Next up, the city-desk

editors. First Grace, ext. 3211, cream, no sugar, followed by Brian Sullivan, ext. 3210, black coffee with a Marlboro red in the parking lot. Jack's assistant; the editorial-page editor; the sports intern; a couple of reporters; and our graphic designer arrive next, in rapid succession. Rocco will be rolling in here soon, and then comes the lull until late afternoon, when most of the reporters and the copy-desk editors start arriving.

AJ is usually late, but he likes to come in through the front door anyway. It's closer to where Alice sits, and he always brings her a hot tea. Everyone else kisses up to the editors, but AJ's the only one who remembers Harry's secretary.

I walk over to Alice now and ask her if the morning mail delivery has arrived.

"Got it right here, hon," she says, pushing the laundry-basket–size container out from under her desk. "Want me to get Jack to carry it for you?"

"It's okay. I've got it."

Alice is a motherly presence in the newsroom. She hounds the reporters to log their hours so they can get paid on time, helps everyone with confusing paperwork, and looks out for the people who work here, especially Harry. She's his rock.

The mailboxes are behind the obit desk, adjacent to the Nerf court. I'm good at the mail. I sort an entire plastic container without stopping to read the names on each mailbox. I'm completely absorbed in the Zen of sorting and about to throw a rather thick press package into Jack's box when a male voice startles me.

"Hi. I don't think we've met."

I turn around to find myself staring at a guy who could very well be the star of some seductive, subtitled film. Dark hair. Blue eyes. Olive skin. *Hello, Rob-McGinty-in-a-few-years.*

"I'm Tony Roma," he says. "The features intern."

Tony Roma? I should be picturing this guy in a powder blue tuxedo with a ruffled shirt singing old Italian songs in a Vegas lounge. At the very least, I should be imagining him plugging his pizzeria chain on local television. And I *would* be picturing those scenarios, if not for the fact that he's so incredibly hot in a universal, *People* magazine's Sexiest Man Alive kind of way. Shelby says some guys just ooze sex, which always sounded gross to me. But that's only because I didn't know what she meant until this exact moment. My body is talking to me. It's telling me things I've never heard it say before—things that warrant a listener-advisory sticker for explicit lyrics.

"Samantha," I say. "Sam I am." I am a total dork.

"Are you the new intern?"

I nod.

"I haven't been around lately. I took time off to cram in an intensive summer class," he says. "Three credits in three weeks."

"Oh," I say. *Oh?*

"Welcome, Sam-I-am," he says, laying a hand on my shoulder. I swear my heart jumps so far, it lands in my inner ear, rendering me off balance. Feeling somewhat light-headed, I return to the obit desk and find AJ already sitting there with a big grin.

"I do not like green eggs and ham," he says.

"Shut up, eavesdropper. You're like an old lady."

"I walked right by you and said hello. *You* didn't hear me."

"I don't think so."

He scowls. "Yeah, well, I see yet another female has fallen victim to the charms of Coma Boy."

"What?! I don't—Coma Boy? What's that supposed to mean?"

"Oh, you know. He's one of these brain-dead guys who wants to be on TV."

"You say that like it's a bad thing." Isn't TV where most people get their news?

"He's a drama major. TV news wouldn't be a bad thing if guys like him would go into acting and leave the news to real reporters."

"I didn't know you felt so passionately about news coverage."

"I don't. I just think he's a dick."

I decide to change the subject. "Michael was here. He asked me to go to city hall with him, but Bernie wouldn't let me. He's going to confront the mayor with what we found out at Bargain Books & Beans."

"You mean what *you* found out, Nancy Drew. Maybe you can invite Coma Boy along on your next fact-finding adventure."

I stick my tongue out at AJ, but his tone stings. I thought our night got better after we left the coffee shop. We walked around town for a while, and as promised, I pointed out everything from Annie Oakley's house to my old dancing school. When he dropped me off at home, AJ told me he'd had fun.

But I don't dwell too much on AJ's dig, because for the rest of the day, I'm completely preoccupied by Tony's mere presence in the newsroom. I search online for articles he's written for the *Herald Tribune*, and I'm slightly disappointed to discover they're all sort of blah. AJ is a much better writer. Oh, well. Tony's an intern too, right? He's bound to improve.

I'd never admit this to anyone, but my lack of focus may be why it's already after nine o'clock (I called my dad two hours ago to tell him I'd be late), we have no feature obit written, and we're totally screwed. I thought AJ made the call; he thought I made the call. Now I'm stuck on the phone with the recently widowed Mrs. Spitaleri, and she just won't give me a break.

"Tell me again why you want to write a story about my husband?" Mrs. Spitaleri asks.

"Because he was a veterinarian, and my editor thinks that's a very interesting profession," I say.

"Why?"

"Well, because not everyone gets to be a veterinarian."

"Not everyone wants to."

She kind of has me there.

I hear AJ in my other ear, enduring a different kind of

obit hell. "How many survivors?" he asks. "Fourteen? Okay, fourteen. Are these all immediate family? Brothers and sisters. Okay. Half? Yes, they count too. Go ahead, I'm ready. Washington, Virginia, Florida, Carolina. Do you realize these first names are all the names of states? Are you sure this is right?"

I turn my attention back to Mrs. S. and try a different approach.

"Are there any interesting stories about your husband that you'd like to share?"

"No."

"Any other interests aside from animals?"

"No. Hard work was his only interest. That's what killed him."

I would have better luck trying to sell her the newspaper. Bernadette is giving me the evil eye, complete with caked-on blue eye shadow—I sense it. So I slouch behind my monitor to avoid her glare.

"Look, honey," Mrs. Spitaleri says, "I know you're just doing your job, but I don't want to answer any of these questions."

Then she hangs up. In about thirty seconds, Bernadette is going to yell, "Moronica, where the hell is my feature obit?" and I have nothing. Maybe the copy desk could just bump up the point size on all the obits? It would serve the dual purpose of filling the page and helping senior citizens— the obit page's most devoted readers, who tend not to be on-line readers. Large-Print Obits. Could be a real selling point.

I try to get AJ's attention to ask him what to do, but he's busy reading back fourteen states' names to some funeral director. If I hang up the phone, Bernadette will pounce. So I keep the receiver propped between my chin and shoulder, pretend to type, and wait for AJ. My head pulses from a caffeine overdose. My contacts feel like Scotch tape on my corneas. This blows. I can't tell Bernadette our feature obit hung up on me. Whose next of kin am I gonna reach at this hour? Full-blown panic is setting in when my phone rings. I hope no one notices I haven't really been on the phone.

"Obit desk," I say. It's my buddy from the Glendale Home for Funerals. He's got news. Good news, sort of. "He did?" I ask. *Really?* God forgive me, I'm giddy with excitement and can't wait to hang up. "Okay, okay. I'll let the city desk know."

Putting the drab green receiver back on the hook, I raise my arms touchdown style and scream, "The police chief of Totowa is dead!" I'm going to hell, but I don't care: We have our feature obit.

"O'Shea! Your police chief is dead!" screams Harry. "Go over there and help D'Angelo write a front-page obit."

Totowa is Meg O'Shea's beat, although she often helps out on big stories like the Paterson fire. As Meg crosses the newsroom toward the obit desk, two thoughts simultaneously enter my brain. Both begin with an expletive. The first is, *Front page? Am I going to write a front-page story?* The second is, *Do I still have to fill the feature slot on the obit page?*

AJ works his mind-meld magic and answers the latter

question. "Don't worry. They can always run a house ad on the obit page," he says. "Plus, they'll have to bump a story or two to make room for the front-page obit."

"Hey, Moron!" Bernadette yells.

"Or Bernie could make me write a feature just for the hell of it. Shit. I'm not missing band practice again," he says. "That old woman is killing my cool."

"Go easy on that *mature* woman," Meg says as she rolls a chair over to my desk. "Hi there. Ready to help me write this story?"

I don't know every reporter yet, but I can tell there are a couple who think talking with interns is beneath them. Meg doesn't fall into that category. She speaks quickly and authoritatively, and I can hear the New Yorker in her. I wish I could be more like her. Confident without being bossy; strong without being bitchy.

"The chief was sick for a long time. I've got most of his obituary written already—we're just looking for react. Let's see," she says, peering at a list of names and numbers she's clutching. "I'll make a copy of this for you. I know his wife, so I'll call her myself. I'll also call the city manager, the acting chief of police, and some of the officers. You can call the city council members. It's late, so I'm not sure who'll be answering their phones. Send me the quotes you get."

Then Meg puts a hand on my shoulder and adds, "Don't worry. After the Paterson fire, this should be easy for you."

It should be, but it's not. I come up empty-handed when I call the first two council members on the list. Both times, I get voice mail and leave a message stating who I am and why I called. Hopefully at least one will call back. I glance over at Tony's desk. The features department looks like a ghost town—desk lamps offs, chairs neatly pushed under desks. I guess writing *Dancing with the Stars* recaps and movie reviews has its advantages. No late-night deadline pressure.

I'm about to phone the third name on the list when I remember something. My neighbor, Mr. Stein, grew up in Totowa. He's mentioned more than once that he and the deceased police chief played ball together in high school. It wouldn't hurt to give him a try while I wait for callbacks from the city council people. I text my dad to tell him I'm going to be even later than I thought and to ask him for Mr. Stein's number, which he provides promptly.

I talk fast when my neighbor picks up. "Hi, Mr. Stein. It's Sam D'Angelo, from next door?" I'm relieved he answered and didn't screen me as a telemarketer when he saw the *Herald Tribune*'s name in his caller ID.

"Sam, how are you, dear? Is everything okay at home?" He sounds concerned.

"Oh, yes, everyone is fine, thanks. I have some bad news, though, about an old buddy of yours, the Totowa chief of police? He passed away tonight."

"Oh, that's too bad. I knew he was sick."

"I was wondering. . . . I'm helping to write his obituary, and I've been asked to gather quotes from people who knew him. Would I be able to ask you a few questions?"

"I'd be happy to help," Mr. Stein says. "Ask away."

Mr. Stein hooks me up with some heartfelt, downright eloquent quotes. After I hang up with him, I'm able to reach the third council member on the list Meg gave me, plus one of the first two returns my call. Not bad.

It's close to eleven by the time I type up my quotes from Mr. Stein and the two town council members. I send them to Meg, who then weaves them into the body of her story. She lets me peer over her shoulder as she puts the finishing touches on her article.

"Nice work getting one of the chief's old school buddies to comment. Where'd you dig him up?"

My face turns crimson. "He's my neighbor. I hope that's okay. I remembered that Mr. Stein knew the chief."

"It's more than okay. He gave us great material," Meg says.

In school, I don't play sports and I'm not in Drama Club or anything, but tonight, I discover for the first time what I've been missing by not being part of something larger than the exclusive clique of me, Shelby, and occasionally Ashley and Caitlin. It's exhilarating working with other people and doing my best work in record time with a deadline looming over my head. Our heads.

AJ checks in with me before he leaves, "Sam-I-am. Need me to wait?"

I'm happy he's not as grumpy as before, and touched that he's starting to feel responsible for me. "I already texted my dad. But thanks." I look him in the eye and try to make it clear that I'm grateful. "See you tomorrow?"

"Same bat time, same bat channel," he says. Then he gives me a quick salute and leaves.

The story finally clears the copy desk around eleven thirty. Even though I know my parents are going to freak about me working so late, it's worth it. It feels like I've won something.

Meg says even though the story will be online tonight, the real payoff for her doesn't happen until the next morning, when she holds the paper in her hands and sips her morning coffee. "And by then everyone has moved on to the next big story." Meg laughs.

But truly, as I leave the newsroom and Harry says, "Not bad, D'Angelo. You haven't screwed anything up yet," it's all the payoff I need.

I'm practically ecstatic—a rare emotion for me—as I walk into our living room with my dad sometime after twelve. I'm about to tell him all about my night (my brain was too fried for speech during the car ride home), but then I see Gram in her recliner. Her eyes are closed, and she's incredibly still. Too still.

chapter six

Home and Garden

Okay, Gram is not dead. What's wrong with me? I realize I had a mental overreaction when I see how unconcerned Dad is as he hovers over Gram and pries the remote from her hand. But for some reason, I'm still standing in the doorway holding my breath as the TV channel guide scrolls and plays light tunes. When Dad shakes her arm lightly, Gram's eyes spring open like she's just emerged from underwater to find herself in a strange place. Only then do I exhale. Dad grabs one of her elbows, and I scoot over to help guide Gram out of the chair. At eighty-one, she's still pretty spry. Probably why, until tonight, I never thought about her dying—not even after Gramps passed away.

I also never spent the summer writing obits before, so there's that.

"Come on, Gram," I say. "I'll walk you upstairs."

"What time is it?" she asks. Her hazel eyes look huge and confused behind her glasses.

"Midnight," I say.

"Gee, this job is making you keep some crazy hours," she says in a loud whisper.

"I know, Gram. But I don't mind."

"Well, at any rate, it's nice to have some late-night company other than the TV for a change," she says. "*Dateline* did a special report about identity theft. Then I watched the news and *Jimmy Kimmel.*"

"Part of *Jimmy Kimmel*, at least," I say.

Gram's a night owl. Unlike my mom, who's up by 5:30 a.m. on weekdays to get an early bus into Manhattan, where she's the editor of the magazine *NYC Lawyer*. Gram's been living with us for the past two years, ever since my grandfather passed away. She has commandeered this TV even though my parents got her a small flat screen for her bedroom. I can tell this bugs my mom. She never complains out loud, but I see her tight smile when she walks through the door after work and gets her usual wave from Gram. Perhaps it has more to do with Gram's constant presence in the living room and less with the unused bedroom TV. It's tough on them all. Gram no longer has her own home, but then again, neither do my parents.

"I'm pretty beat," Dad says. "I fell asleep before the news. I hope these late nights aren't going to be a pattern."

"You should talk," I joke. "Maybe your rock-and-roll lifestyle is catching up with you."

In addition to being a lawyer, my dad's the bassist for the Breakfast Club, named for the John Hughes film. My parents *love* all things '80s, especially the music, even the cheesy one-hit wonders. Like me. I, too, am a one-hit wonder, though I wouldn't call myself cheesy.

"I contributed to a front-page story tonight," I say.

"You did? That's great! That should have been the first thing you told me," Dad said. "You buried the lead."

"Quit using newsroomspeak. Anyway, the front-page story *is* an obit. The police chief of Totowa died. I'll probably get a tag line. No big deal."

My nonchalant facade doesn't fool my dad. He understands my supreme indifference is my way of not letting the universe know how badly I want something for fear of jinxing it. Unlike a lot of sixteen-year-olds, in addition to loving my parents, I like them. They get me. Most of the time, though, I worry that I'm disappointing them. I picture Mom and Dad talking about me in bed at night, discussing, in hushed whispers, how the cool gene managed to skip a generation and wondering aloud if I'll turn out okay.

"Obit or not, I'll be looking forward to seeing that story tomorrow," Dad says, kissing the top of my head. We're one of the few families on the block who still get the paper delivered. Gram likes to work the crossword puzzle at breakfast.

"Good night, Dad."

Gram shuffles along, and I steer her toward the steps.

"Come on, Gram," I say. "Show a little hustle, will you? I'm exhausted."

Gram and I snipe at each other a lot. We both appreciate caustic humor.

"You'll be happy if you have half my hustle when you're my age."

When we finally reach Gram's room, my eyes settle on a picture of Gramps she keeps on her nightstand. He's wearing his glasses and a sweater vest. He's also smiling and waving. Whenever I look at the photo, it always feels like he's waving to me from where he is now, not where he was when the photo was taken, which was beside my grandmother at their dining room table on Christmas.

"So, *Dateline* did a thing on identity theft?" I ask as I bend down to kiss my Gram on the cheek.

"Did you know 2.5 million dead people are victims of identity theft every year? It's modern-day grave robbing," she says, clearly quoting the show. "The program was edifying."

Gram has an amazing vocabulary, and English isn't even her first language. Her parents emigrated from Italy, and they spoke Italian at home. Gram didn't go to college, but she's well read, curious, and probably the smartest person I know. She uses a pen for even the most complex crossword puzzles and keeps a dictionary and thesaurus by her bed, next to Gramps's photo.

"I guess it wouldn't be *so* bad if someone steals my identity when I die."

"Gram! Why would you say that?"

"I won't need it anymore. It will be like I'm living forever."

As I walk to my room, as much as I wish Gram will live forever, I can't stop myself from imagining a day when Gram, too, is smiling and waving at me in a photograph from a place that isn't here. My brain is ear-to-ear morbid tonight. Add the five Diet Cokes I drank today to worries about Gram and lingering dead-police-chief excitement, and it's like the perfect storm for insomnia.

I'm also beginning to see the newsroom in my dreams. It reminds me of when I was younger and we'd spend an entire day at the beach. I always dove into the water as soon as we got there and rode the waves for hours with my green Boogie board. After those marathon beach days, I'd lie in bed still feeling the ocean lifting me up, suspending me atop a wave and dropping me down again. It's the kind of tired I love, then and now.

Before I finally drift off, I think about helping Meg with the police-chief story and how quickly things get done when time is running out. If teams can win national championships with less than ten seconds on the clock, surely I can run six miles outside, help Michael figure out what's going on with the mysterious Sy Goldberg, and get a guy like Tony to notice me before school starts in September. Deadlines. They make things happen. I officially set mine for the last day of summer.

chapter seven

Front Page

My ringing cell phone wakes me. I crack one eye and look at the screen, Shelby. "Wha?" I mumble.

"Your name is on the front page of the paper!" she yells. She sounds excited. I can't believe she's (a) awake and (b) reading. Shelby seeking information or knowledge is not something I'm used to. "It's not the first name listed—it's under Megan O'Shea's name—but it's still there," she says. "I guess it's more like half a byline?" I love her, but Shelby's never going to be on *Jeopardy!*

"If it were half a byline, it would just say 'Samantha' or 'D'Angelo,'" I clarify for her. I'm already jogging down the steps to the kitchen. "I'm gonna go check it out. Call you back."

I'd only been expecting a tag line—my name in small print at the end of the story. It was very cool of Meg to share her byline. When I get downstairs, Gram, the consummate obit reader, could not be prouder.

"Well, if it isn't Scoop D'Angelo!" she booms as she reaches for the coffeepot. She's wearing pale blue capri pants, white Keds, and a cotton top with a glittery floral print—Gram likes some bling. Her youthful getup erases the nagging image from the previous night.

"Oh, Gram," I say, giving her a hug.

"Nice job on that obituary," she says. "I already called Aunt Jo and Aunt Connie. They read it too."

I pick up the paper and take in the image of my name. Samantha D'Angelo. Meg's right. It feels better to hold it in my hands.

"Cool," I say. But inside, I'm turning cartwheels and clicking my heels. (Not that I've ever *actually* clicked my heels. Does anyone who's three-dimensional and not on the Cartoon Network?)

How could I not know I've always wanted this? Seeing my name on the front page is so much better than seeing it on the obit page. I imagine this is how it would have felt to see my name on a callback list for all the things I tried out for but never made—the school play (twice), girls' choir, the softball and bowling teams, and the cheerleading squad (I never had a chance at that last one; it was Mom's idea). Could it be I'm better on paper?

"Is Dad working from home today?" I ask Gram.

Lucky for me, my dad telecommutes most days.

"Yep. He's been on a conference call for an hour," Gram says.

"Good. I need a ride to work," I say.

"Aunt Connie is picking me up. We're getting our hair done. We can give you a lift if you want."

I picture myself adrift in the back seat of Aunt Connie's 1999 Lincoln Town Car, coming in for a landing, complete with screeching wheels, in front of the *Herald Tribune*.

"I'll stick with Dad," I say. "But you be careful driving around with that Aunt Connie. She drives like she's in London, only she's not. Remember, stay to the right. It's the first rule of the road in the state of New Jersey. You keep telling her that."

"I know, I know. I wish I'd learned to drive years ago. Now I'm stuck," she says. "Come to think of it, if she gets any more points on her license, I'll be stuck again—for good!"

"Not if I get my license in August."

Gram raises her eyebrows. I leave her to imagine the possibilities, and carry the paper up to my room to read the story again. Every quote is heartfelt and genuine. *"He became a police officer because he believed in changing people's lives for the better." "You couldn't ask for a more dedicated chief. He was a leader, but more than that, he really cared."* The article concludes with Mr. Stein's quote. *"He exuded confidence. The kind of guy who could do anything he set his mind to."*

The chief was loved, that's for sure. A lifelong Totowa resident, in high school he was student council president and an all-state pitcher. After graduating magna cum laude from Rutgers, he entered the police academy and eventually joined the Totowa force. As he worked his way up the ranks, he earned a law degree at night.

In addition to a recent photo, the *Herald Tribune* ran an old picture of him on the pitcher's mound, high-fiving the catcher after a big win. Was the chief confident because he was successful, or successful because he was confident? It's like some people just know how to hit the switch and turn their lives on faster than others.

I mull this over while I try to decide between going for a run and climbing back under the covers. Before I can make up my mind, my cell plays the alt-rock song AJ downloaded as my new ring tone. I'm still staring at the paper when I answer my phone.

"What?"

"Is that how you talk to the woman who pays your cell phone bills?"

"Mom, sorry. I thought you were Shelby again."

"Great job on the story, hon. Front page! We're so proud of you."

"Thanks, Mom," I say.

"Let's try to eat dinner as a family when you get home. I haven't seen you in days," she says. "I'm not sure I like you working these late hours."

"I don't mind it. I like what I'm doing."

"I'm glad you do, sweetie. But I miss you."

"Miss you too," I say. I barely have time to disconnect before my phone rings again. I look at the screen. This time it is Shelby.

"Hello?"

"You were supposed to call me back."

"You didn't give me a chance."

"We should celebrate your story. Let's hit the pool."

"I can't. I have to work."

Shelby sighs. "You haven't been to the pool once since school let out."

"I know, I know." For a split second, I feel nostalgic for our old summer routine. Shelby and I have logged a lot of hours at the community pool. "Maybe I'll get there this weekend."

"How about tonight? Let's do something."

"I'm working late. How about tomorrow night?"

"Okaaay," Shelby says. I hear her pouting through the phone. I try to smooth things over.

"What happened with Hollister? Maybe you should apply to a few other places in case that job doesn't come through. How about the shoe store?"

"Sam," Shelby sighs. "Unlike you, I don't exactly mind not having a summer job."

Two roads diverge in the woods—I take one and Shelby takes the other. Or maybe Shelby sits down on a rock and relaxes. I almost laugh out loud.

"Call you later," I say, and then I hang up and reach for my running shoes.

———

L ater that day, at work, I cut out my first front-page story and put it in my top desk drawer, where I also placed Anton's obituary. When I look up, Tony is sitting on the corner of the obit desk. I nearly fall out of my chair, and my stomach does a back handspring.

"Front page!" he says. "Nice."

"Thanks." My face is on fire. I wonder if I look like I'm having an allergic reaction.

AJ gives me a strange look as he passes behind Tony en route from Alice's desk to the mailboxes, the giant U.S. Postal container in hand.

"Come on," Tony says. "I'm going to the deli. Let me buy you a congratulatory coffee."

"Okay." I don't particularly want or need coffee, but I can't help it. Before I know it, I'm following him out of the newsroom like a sheep.

"Going to the deli," I say to AJ as I walk toward the exit with Tony. "Want anything?"

He never looks my way, just continues to sort mail. A few awkward seconds tick away. Finally he says, "Nope. I'm good."

On our way back to the *Herald Tribune*, Tony and I run into Tessie. She's another regular at John's Corner Deli. I see her most afternoons. She's carrying her pink motorcycle helmet—the one that matches her Harley-Davidson parked at the curb.

"Hey, Tessie," I say. "Taking a break from deliveries?"

She laughs. "I need my afternoon cup of joe," she says.

Tessie's a riot. She's got to be close to seventy, and she still rides around on her Harley delivering Avon. She told me she got bored with retirement and went into cosmetics sales.

"She'd make a great profile," I say to Tony as we stroll down the sidewalk. "I was going to ask Jack if I could work on it."

"You should. He'll let you. You're like the newsroom wunderkind," he says, nudging me lightly with his shoulder.

The sudden contact sends my heart rate straight into the aerobic zone. "No, I'm not," I insist. "I hardly did anything. It was all Meg."

"Don't be so modest," he says. "I've been thinking of asking Harry to let me cover more hard news. My adviser thinks I need some stronger pieces for my portfolio."

"You should," I say. "I'm sure he'd let you."

Tony grimaces. "Well, that makes one of us. I'm not his favorite person."

"I don't believe that."

"It's true," Tony says as he holds open the side door for me.

Does Harry not like Tony? I'm not sure what to say, so I keep my mouth shut as I step into the dimly lit stairwell. It's one flight up to the newsroom.

"Thanks again for the coffee," I say.

"No problem. If you come to bar night, I'll buy you a beer," Tony says just before we go through the newsroom door.

"Bar night?"

"Yeah, at the Harp & Bard. Every Wednesday. Sometimes Thursday. Didn't anyone tell you?"

"No." I feel the familiar pang of being left out.

"Try to make it. Everyone usually heads over right after work," he says.

"Maybe," I say, trying to sound casual, and wondering if I'll need a fake ID.

"Oh, come on, you can do better than 'maybe,'" he says, and does that shoulder-bump thing again. "The first round is on me."

Is he flirting with me? Maybe he's this way with everyone.

"I'll try," I say. Out of the corner of my eye, I see AJ watching us.

"You'd better do more than try."

"Thanks again for the coffee."

I stride toward the obit desk, intent on laying into AJ for not telling me about bar nights, when I'm intercepted by Meg.

"Great job on that obit, kiddo," she says.

"I hardly did anything," I say. "Thank you for the byline. That was awesome."

"You know, Harry will never say this to you," she says, leaning toward me, "but he was very impressed by how you handled yourself on deadline. If I were you, I'd show a little chutzpah and ask him if you can cover some spot news, or maybe even a council meeting or two. It's summer. Reporters will be looking for vacation coverage."

My mind immediately jumps to Michael's beat. I've been researching other public corruption cases in New Jersey in my free time. (I should be getting gel manicures like

Shelby, but at least I'm aware of my nerdy ways.) Kickback schemes, embezzlement of county funds, tax evasion; it's unfortunate, but there are countless examples of how our elected officials abuse the public's trust. A common thread running through a lot of these cases is that reporters are usually the first to uncover the corruption. *We are the watchdogs*, I've heard Harry say. Even then, it takes years for the authorities to bring these people to justice. Michael is honing in on Sy Goldberg as a starting point. Finding him is just the beginning; who knows where it could lead?

"Do you think Harry will let me cover real news?"

"Absolutely," she says. "But even if he says no, Harry appreciates aggressive writers."

"Thanks, Meg. For everything."

I finally settle into my desk chair and tap my keyboard, bringing my computer screen to life.

"Nice of you to grace us with your presence," AJ says. "Ready to do some work, or are you going to milk the police-chief obit accolades for the rest of the day?"

Why is he being such a jerk? I'm racking my brain for a razor-sharp comeback, but I've got nothin'. The obit phone rings, and for once I'm thrilled. I snatch the receiver. "Obit desk, can I help you?" It comes out louder and angrier than I intended. "Sure. How many do you have?"

I start typing and vow to ignore AJ for the rest of the afternoon.

Around dinnertime, I plop a Snapple carton filled with orders on the obit desk. AJ is on the phone and doesn't look up. We still haven't spoken. I sneak a peek in Tony's direction and see Alexis, one of the *Herald Tribune*'s photographers or photogs, leaning her butt against Tony's desk, with her long, thin legs stretched out before her. Tony's tilting back in his chair, hands behind his head like he's about to do a crunch, and smiling up at her as she relates what must be some wildly interesting anecdote involving her and her five-foot-nine, size-double-zero friends.

At that very moment, I vow to start wearing makeup and use a blow dryer instead of always wrapping my long hair in a careless twist. I slump into my seat. What was I thinking? Why would he flirt with me when girls like Alexis so obviously flirt with him? Maybe there's something going on between them. I'll find a subtle way to ask AJ about it, if he'll talk to me. In the meantime, I've got dinner orders to distribute.

I take the box with me and purposely wait to give AJ his roast beef sub last.

"What's going on between Tony and Alexis?" I blurt out as I hand him his sandwich.

"Are you starting a *Herald Tribune* gossip blog? Cool. Our lame-ass website needs *something*," AJ says, nonplussed. "How should I know who Coma Boy is doing these days? At times it seems like his life's ambition is to work his way through every chick in the newsroom."

"Aren't you afraid he's going to hear you calling him that?" I ask.

"In addition to being stupid, he's so arrogant he'd never think I was talking about him. Why are you so interested, anyway?" he says, and then, much to my horror, starts singing, "Sam and Tony sitting in a tree . . ."

"What's wrong with you?!" I whisper-scream. "Shut up!"

AJ laughs and slaps the desk. "I don't think I've sung that song since first grade. It was worth it to see the panic on your face."

"Don't talk to me," I say. "Why don't you go call Jessica or something?"

"Oh, now you're mad at me for one little joke?" he asks.

"No, I'm mad at you because you're an idiot and because you never told me about bar nights," I say.

"Did Coma Boy mention bar night?" he asks.

"Yes, *Tony* did," I say.

"Figures," he says.

"Why didn't you tell me?"

"Uh, listen, Totally Underage Girl, it's not exactly my thing. Anyway, I usually have band practice."

"Oh, so, because *you* don't go, *I* shouldn't go."

"I never said that. I just don't give bar nights much thought," he says.

"You don't seem to give *anything* much thought," I say, and immediately feel bad for the dig.

"Whatever," he says.

"*Whatever,*" I mimic like a big baby, and stomp over to Jack's desk to pick up a bunch of press releases. I carry them back to my desk and start sorting them. After a few silent minutes, during which I try not to look at AJ or Tony and pretend to be terribly engrossed in writing Community Calendar blurbs, AJ is the first to speak again.

"So, what did he say about bar night?"

"That I should go," I say. "That he'll buy me a beer."

"He's such a dog."

"We should both go sometime. If you don't have a band thing," I say. I almost add, *Or a girlfriend thing*, because, it occurs to me, I *still* don't know where AJ stands with that Jessica person. But I don't want him mad at me again, so I leave the girl part out.

"So, now you're using me for a ride? Nice." He's smiling, though, in his subtle AJ way, so I know he's only joking. Earlier today, I wasn't so sure.

"You *know* I don't drive, and I can't ask my mom or dad to pick me up from work and drop me off at a bar," I say. "Anyway, it will be more fun if you're there."

"I'll think about it. I'm warning you, though. If we go, I'm going to tell everyone you begged me to take you."

"Whatever," I say as Alexis once again arrives at Tony's desk. Shouldn't she be out taking photos?

Sometime before lunch, I must have sprung a slow leak, because all the excitement I felt when I walked in here this morning has slowly seeped out of me.

chapter eight

Special Investigation

"**K**idney stones."

That's what AJ says when I ask him if anyone's heard from Michael. I waited for him all day yesterday, but he never came in. I've been dying to find out what happened on Monday when he confronted the mayor about Sy Goldberg being his coffee-shop partner.

"What do you mean?"

"Michael has kidney stones."

"Is it serious?"

"To Michael. They're a bitch to pass."

"Pass? Huh? Is he going to call in again?"

"Why?"

"I want to find out what happened at city hall yesterday."

"Tell Harry you want to talk to Michael when he calls."

"Good idea."

I do a quick check of Harry's hair. When he's stressed, Harry runs both hands through his curly locks like he's rinsing shampoo. When he takes his hands out, his hair stays put at the new, higher elevation. Looks like I'm in the clear. I walk to the city desk, where's he's sitting in front of a computer.

"Uh, Harry?"

"D'Angelo."

"If Michael calls in today, can I speak to him?"

"Sure," he says without looking away from whatever he's reading.

"Thanks."

That was easy. May as well go for it.

"Harry?"

"D'Angelo."

"Meg mentioned to me that you sometimes need people to fill in for vacationing reporters."

"Yep."

"Well, uh, I was wondering, when Michael goes away this summer, do you think maybe . . ."

"Spit it out, D'Angelo."

I say it so fast, my words blur together. "Do you think Icouldcoverforhim?"

This gets his attention. He looks up at me.

"Say that again?"

"Do you think I could cover for him?"

"You do know it's one of our most important beats?"

"I do. But I've been doing research, and I even tried to help Michael by visiting the coffee shop, and—"

"You're not the first intern to call dibs on Michael's beat, you know."

"I'm not?" Did AJ ask Harry about it?

"But it's possible you're more qualified than the other applicant. I'll think about it."

I'm beaming. "You will?"

"I just said so, didn't I? Now get back to work. I can find some filing cabinets for you to clean if we're not keeping you busy enough."

"I'm good, thanks."

I scurry back to the death desk before he makes good on his threat.

"Hey," I say to AJ. "Did you ask Harry about covering for Michael this summer?"

"Why the heck would I do that?"

"Just checking. I asked Harry about it. He said another intern was also interested. I wouldn't want to stand in your way."

"It's either Coma Boy or the sports intern."

Of all the ways I've envisioned Tony, "the competition" wasn't on the list.

Late in the afternoon, I get a text from Shelby alluding to the fact that I never called her back yesterday.

Forget something?

I pick up the phone and call her.

"Nice of you to remember your best friend."

"Sorry, I forgot."

"So. Can you go out *tonight*?"

Do I feel like going out with Shelby? I'm about to answer when Harry screams my name and points to the phone receiver in his hand.

"Gotta run. Call you back."

I hang up on Shelby to free my line.

"I've got Michael," Harry says. He transfers the call, and my phone rings a second later.

"Michael, how are you?"

"Awful. I'll be better once I pass these things," he says. *Pass these things.* I'm not completely clear about what that means, but it doesn't sound good.

"How'd it go at city hall on Monday?"

"I never got there. The pain hit on the ride over."

I'm disappointed. It's too bad about the kidney stones and all, but still, I was looking forward to hearing all about it.

"But I did call the mayor this morning," Michael says.

"That's great! What happened?"

"I asked him how Sy, his new *business partner*, is doing. And he says, 'Not good. I'm going to see him after work.'"

"Where? Is Sy in the hospital?" I ask.

"That's what I asked him. He said it was none of my business and hung up on me."

"What are you going to do?"

"I'm going to call some local hospitals, see if any Sy Goldbergs have been admitted."

"Can they confirm that for you?"

"Some hospitals are better about giving information to reporters than others," Michael says. "Short of following him, it's the best I can do."

Michael keeps talking about how validating the mayor's claims that Sy is sick would at least give his story some credibility blah, blah, blah. But I stop paying close attention after the words "following him."

How cool would that be? I would love to help Michael with another lead while he's incapacitated.

"Feel better, Michael," I say when he's finished speaking. "Hope everything, uh . . . passes well."

My head is spinning with questions when I get off the phone.

Why would Mayor Amato start a new business with a dying man? What is he getting out of his partnership with Sy Goldberg? Money, I suppose. Was the mayor forced to invest in the coffee shop as some kind of quid pro quo for Sy getting a cushy job with the city?

I've got to help Michael find Sy. I stare at AJ until he looks up from his computer.

"What?"

"What are you doing later?" I ask.

"Is this about bar night, because—"

"No, no, I mean earlier than that—like, five o'clock."

AJ eyes me suspiciously. Who could blame him?

"Uh, working here?"

I give AJ my *duh* look.

"I need your help with something."

"A ride for the dinner run?" he asks.

"No. But that's a good cover."

"Cover? For what?"

"Do you know what Michael's mayor looks like?" I say.

"Sure. I've covered my share of weekend ribbon cuttings in his town."

"Cool. I'll take food orders, and we'll leave after that. We should have enough time to get everything done."

"I didn't hear myself agree to help you with anything," AJ says.

"Will you?"

"No."

"Please?"

"What's in it for me?"

"Good karma?"

"I need something more tangible."

"I'll pay for your dinner?"

"Not good enough," AJ says.

"And write the feature obits for the rest of the week?"

"Done. Hand me the Sunny Garden menu."

———

We pull up a block away from East Passaic city hall. Luckily, the mayor has a special parking space in front for his Jaguar. This should make it easier. I'm feeling jittery, partly because I don't do sneaky well. I'm wearing my sunglasses. I make AJ do the same and hand him the never-worn Zildjian baseball cap I found lying on the passenger-side floor. Probably got it for free the last time he bought cymbals or drumsticks. My dad has a Fender one just like it.

"I don't do hats," he says, trying to push it away.

"Just deal. We're on a stakeout."

"You need to get a grip, Sam-I-am."

It's ten to five. AJ and I left the newsroom at four thirty to pick up our Sunny Garden order. The smell of Chinese food is now pervading AJ's Jeep. Ugh. General Tso's chicken smells better in less confined spaces. Hopefully, we'll be able to tail the mayor and get back to the newsroom before anyone notices how long we've been gone and the food gets cold. I did tell Meg what we're up to. She's on deadline but said she'll try to cover the phones for me as much as possible.

Five minutes later, the mayor walks down the steps of city hall and gets into his car. He makes an illegal U-turn on Main Street and leaves us facing the wrong direction.

"Turn the car around!" I yell.

"Listen, CSI Girl. I'm doing the best I can."

By the time AJ points us in the right direction, we're a good three car lengths behind the mayor.

"Oh, I wish I had binoculars."

"What the hell do you need binoculars for? The mayor's car is right there. It's not like we're at sea."

"Right. Because that's the *only* time people use binoculars."

"Just sayin'. People don't usually drive around in broad daylight with them."

"Okay, okay. Just focus."

Two blocks later, a city bus pulls in front of us.

"Oh, no! Go around. Go around. I can't see him."

"I suppose now you wish you had X-ray vision," AJ says.

The bus stops at the next corner, and we're able to pass it and get close to the mayor's car again. At the next corner, he pulls into a bank parking lot and drives up to the ATM. We stay a car length behind but pretend we're waiting for the cash machine as well. "The machine looks like it spit out a wad of cash," AJ says. After the bank, we tail him for twenty-five minutes, during which we pass both St. Matthew's Hospital and Passaic County General. Then the mayor gets on Route 21. Where is he going?

"He's getting on the highway," AJ says. "We can't keep following him."

"Just for a little while longer, please?"

AJ sighs and puts his blinker on. We cruise down Route 21, keeping a safe distance, and follow the mayor through three towns before he exits the highway. About a mile down the road, the mayor pulls into Fidelity Savings and parks. AJ pulls into a space a row from the mayor's car. We watch him go inside. I consider following him but don't know what that would accomplish. We wait in silence for a while. It's taking forever.

"Why does he bank here?" I ask.

"Good interest rates?"

"Let's see where he goes."

"Let's not," AJ says. "It's getting late. Someone's going to miss us soon."

"But maybe he's going to one of the hospitals after the bank. Or to Sy's house," I say, more to myself than to AJ.

"Listen, Miss Daisy, maybe we should head back to the office and leave the detective work to people who know what the frig they're doing," AJ says. He sounds annoyed, but it's hard to take him seriously in that hat. I can see why he doesn't wear them. He really does look stupid, especially with his ponytail all smushed.

"Fine." It's AJ's car. I can't argue. Plus, I don't want him feeling like my chauffeur. I lean forward and try to catch his gaze.

"Thanks. For helping me out. For always helping me out," I say.

He takes his eyes off the road to look at me. I think he's going to say something, but he just gives me a half smile and shakes his head.

"What?"

"Nothin'."

We're both quiet for the rest of the ride.

When we get back to the *Herald Tribune*, we're pretty much screwed thanks to me. We're barraged by complaints that the hot-and-sour soup is cold, the obit calls have been piling up, and neither of us bothered to sort the mail today.

"Don't even think about going to the Harp tonight," AJ says.

I had forgotten all about it—*almost*. I'm already feeling silly about following the mayor around while he did his banking. I wish AJ hadn't mentioned it. Full-blown grouch-iness is imminent. Alexis will probably be there flirting her skirt off with Tony, and I'll be missing out.

"I'm really not dressed to go out anyway," I say. It's the truth.

"It's the Harp. Who cares? Oh, wait, that's right, your *boyfriend* is going to be there," AJ says.

"I smell like Chinese food, and I'm feeling too schleppy to go anywhere with anyone," I snap.

"And I should feel sorry for you because . . . ? Have you seen what that hat did to my hair?"

I choke back a laugh and get to work. For the next two hours, AJ and I play catch-up. As promised, I write the feature, pulling together the best story I can while finishing up the rest of the obits and sending them over to the copy desk. Admittedly, I'm not very focused. My mind is occu-pied with thoughts of the mayor, Tony, and Alexis. Plus, the egg roll I gobbled down feels like a tennis ball in my stom-ach. Oh, and I forgot to call Shelby. Darn it. I want to take the gutless way out and text her, but I owe her a quick call.

"Hey," I say when she picks up the phone.

"Finally," she says. "You were supposed to call me back hours ago."

"I'm sorry. Things got really busy."

"You say that a lot since you got this job. Wait . . . is

this about a guy? Are you crushing on someone at work?" She sounds hopeful.

"What? No. I'm just busy."

Of course little miss I'm-gonna-ditch-my-girlfriends-for-a-hot-guy-from-Düsseldorf would assume it's about a boy. But I don't want to get into it right now.

"I'm sooo bored," Shelby whines. "Please say we're going out tonight."

"If you had a job, you wouldn't be bored."

"If I had a job, *I'd* still want to go out."

"It's not that I don't want to, I can't. I'm working later than I thought. But I'm off on Friday. We'll go to the pool then. All day."

"Swear?"

"Swear."

It's like talking to a five-year-old. I hang up the phone and start typing.

Shelby Thorpe, 91, died today. Born with a rare condition called Etch A Sketch brain, it was difficult for her to retain vital information or hold a regular job. She is preceded in death by her first three husbands and survived by her fiancé, William Barclay, of the Sunrise assisted living center in Chestnutville.

Select all. Delete. I've got to find that girl a job. But right now all I want to do is go home, wash the smell of General Tso's chicken out of my hair, and collapse into bed.

chapter nine

Retraction

AJ saunters into the *Herald Tribune* newsroom as he usually does— exactly ten minutes late. His tardiness is nothing if not consistent. He pulls his earbuds out and plops down at his desk facing mine. It's been a bad morning, and I've been on edge waiting for him to get here.

"Finally," I say.

"Sam-I-am. Why the frown?"

"You don't wanna know."

"Uh, yeah, I do."

"You're going to laugh at me."

"It's what I live for. What'd ya do? Follow the mayor to the men's room?"

"I accidentally switched the name of a deceased man with that of his very alive, very angry son in the feature obit that ran in today's paper," I say.

"Was his name Mark Twain?"

AJ can be so enigmatic. I throw up my hands and give him a WTF look.

"What? Mark Twain's obit ran while he was still alive. Google it. Better yet, Bing it. I'm trying to start a revolution."

"Okay. So, you're not helping me."

"Were their names at least close, like a senior and a junior?"

"Nope. The son called and screamed his head off. Of course Bernadette took the call and wasted no time ratting me out to Harry."

"You pissed off Harry and Bernie in one morning?" he says. "Nice. Do you even think about the rest of us?"

I can't shake the feeling of, as AJ would put it, "getting ripped a new butthole" by the grieving yet very pissed-off, son. It's a small consolation to think that, in a bizarre way, I took his mind off his loss. Bernadette transferred the son's call to me and made me apologize. Since then, my anxiety has been building, anticipating when Harry's going to call me into his office and chew me out.

"My chances at covering for Michael in August are slipping away," I say.

"Look at it this way: At least Harry doesn't know about our mayoral stakeout."

AJ's right. Following the mayor threw my entire afternoon off. I was all frazzled when we got back. It seems so ridiculous now. Harry would be doubly pissed to know the reason behind my carelessness.

Out of the corner of my eye, I see Tony heading in my

general direction and am reminded that I've already broken my vow to wear makeup and style my hair every day.

"Hey, Sam, AJ. How's it goin'?" Tony looks back and forth between us. "Am I interrupting?"

"No, no. Not at all," I say.

"Feel like taking a walk?" Tony says to me. "I need another coffee."

My stomach feels like I'm riding a roller coaster and careening down the first big drop. As much as I want to go, I can't. I've had enough trouble for one day. I need to concentrate.

"I should stay put."

"Can I get you anything?"

"What? Uh, no. Thanks. I'm all set."

"Okay, then. Just thought I'd ask."

Then he smiles at me, and I come very close to changing my mind. As Tony walks away, AJ calls after him, "No, I didn't want anything either. Thank you!" Then he says quietly, so Tony won't hear, "Coma Boy."

To AJ's surprise, Tony turns around. "Oh, sorry, man. Did you need something?" He's being genuinely nice, AJ's sarcasm apparently lost on him.

"No, thanks," AJ says.

We're swamped for the rest of the day. In addition to obits, website blurbs, movie timetables, phone calls, and food runs, AJ and I are putting together a Fourth of July roundup of all the events happening this weekend. Before I know it, it's six o'clock.

Even with all the multitasking going on, I've been extra

diligent about getting every obit right. Thankfully, we've got plenty to fill the page. No feature tonight—Yes! Harry still hasn't talked to me about my big blunder, but the nagging inside me is fading. Hard work, like running, gives me a rush.

"D'Angelo!" Bernadette squawks from across the room.

My bubble of optimism pops.

"Wow, she used your *name*," AJ says. "She must really be pissed."

What did I do wrong? I've been triple-checking obit names all day. I hope I didn't misspell a word. It's never enough for her to beckon me over to the copy desk and tell me which word I spelled wrong; she likes to grab the dictionary that sits on her computer, flip to the page with the word in question, and point it out to me with her yellowed fingernail. I usually try to hide my impatience so that the didactic exercise need not take any longer than necessary.

But Bernadette is even more animated than usual. She's waving both arms above her head, and I feel vaguely like a jet being directed into the terminal at Newark Liberty Airport. Then she gets up to meet me halfway between the obit desk and the copy desk, which puts us right in front of the city desk.

"EFFFF, Whyyyyy, Eyyyyyee!!!" she says when she's about two inches away from my face.

I know I'm going to faint from the combination of embarrassment and her awful coffee breath.

"It is not *Rally*, North Carolina. It is *Raleigh!*"

Bernadette hails from somewhere south of the Mason-Dixon Line and until tonight, I was never sure where. I guess I hit her right in the hometown with my recent egregious error. Sadly, between her anger and her accent, which has returned with a vengeance, both words are sounding exactly the same to me. But I'm smart enough to keep my mouth shut. Perhaps she reads the persistent confusion on my face, though, because suddenly she begins yelling and spelling at the same time.

"That's R-A-L-E-I-G-H, Moronica!"

Grace, the kindest of the city-desk editors, pushes herself away from her terminal and is about to come to my rescue. "Just a minute, Bernie," she says, but she's interrupted by an event that really raises the bar on the sentence "I had a bad day at work." Grace hasn't even lifted her backside from the chair before Bernadette clutches her chest and her face turns a shade of red that truly brings to mind blood boiling. She begins taking wheezing, labored breaths.

"I need to sit," she whispers.

Harry wastes no time rolling a chair in her direction and guiding her into the sitting position. Jack is on the spot with bottled water. Grace fans Bernie's face and administers calm advice. "Take deep, even breaths, Bernie. Deep, even breaths."

OhmyGod. Is she having a heart attack?

"Relax, Bernie," Harry says. "Are you okay? Should I dial nine-one-one?"

Bernie shakes her head. "Just hand me that water."

I back up slowly, bringing my hands up to my face and covering my eyes. I'm not sure what to do. Is Bernie going to be okay? Does she need to go to the ER? This is all my fault. I want to help Bernie, but I'm afraid. It feels like the music has stopped and I don't have a chair.

I'm about to cry and don't want to do it in front of everyone. I look from my desk to the restroom, and then I do the only thing I can think of. I run. Across the length of the newsroom and straight through the double doors leading to the pressroom. I make a sharp right once I get inside and look for a place to hide. I spot the giant spools of paper, like overgrown rolls of paper towels, and head their way. I slink between two of them, press my back to the cinder-block wall, and slide my butt to the ground. My face is feverishly hot, and I'm sure my nervous splotches are abounding.

I look up at the presses, a roller-coaster-like network of conveyor belts that snake through the warehouse. It reminds me of a megasize version of that old board game *Mousetrap*. The bay doors to the loading dock are open. A tempting escape.

Tears stream silently down my face, and my nose starts running. What did I do? Why didn't I just hold it together? I'm thinking about how badly I need a tissue when a pair of black Converse shuffle into my sight line. AJ. He doesn't offer me a tissue, just a hand. I put mine in his and allow him to pull me up, and then he does something I totally don't expect. He draws me close to his chest and wraps his arms around me. I curl into him. My tears fall against his

AC/DC T-shirt. My thoughts are wavering between *This should be awkward but it's not* and *Wow, AJ is solid.*

Finally, AJ breaks the embrace and says, "Are you done being all girly and emotional?"

That gets one corner of my mouth to turn up. "I think so. But I can't go back in there."

"Let's do a few jumping jacks first."

"What are you talking about?"

Oh, no, he isn't. But yes, there he is, doing jumping jacks between the rolls of unused newspaper.

"Come on. Do them with me. No one can be unhappy when they're doing jumping jacks."

I don't know why. Maybe because I know he's doing this for me, but I start doing jumping jacks too. First I smile. Then I laugh. We're both cracking up when pressman Franco walks up, gut hanging over his belt, and gives us a long look. "Call me when it's time for Pilates," he says. And then he walks away.

"Ready to go back?" AJ asks, a little out of breath. "Don't sweat it. Bernie's going to be fine. Jack took her home."

"AJ, I still can't."

AJ puts his hands on his hips and looks around. "Okay, then. Follow me."

I do as he says as he walks toward the open bay doors, but I freeze when he jumps down into the loading zone.

"Jump," he says.

"It's too high."

"It's only, like, four or five feet."

"So am I."

"Come on. Don't be a chicken. Let's get out of here."

"I can't leave. I need my stuff."

"Sit down. I'll be right back." Then he jogs toward the front of the building.

I turn around to make sure no one is watching, then plop down on the edge of the loading dock. AJ comes back a few minutes later, my bag and phone in hand. He puts them on the ground and walks toward me.

"Here, give me your hands."

I put both my hands in his.

"Now jump," he says. "I've got you."

I push off and land on my feet. AJ never lets go. We stand that way for a few seconds, just looking at each other.

"AJ, I—"

When I start to speak, he abruptly drops my hands.

"Come on. I'll drive you home."

"Oh, yeah. Thanks." I pick up my bag and my phone. "I was gonna say . . . that's the nicest thing anyone has ever done for me."

"Sam-I-am, it's time you started living."

Then he smiles, and it's like I'm jumping off the loading dock all over again.

chapter ten

Puzzles

I don't even pretend sleep is an option tonight. My thoughts vacillate between my almost-moment with AJ and the unfortunate incident with Bernie that led us to the *Herald Tribune*'s loading dock to begin with.

AJ was his usual self on the ride home. He played some tracks by a band he's into, and by the time we got to my house, it was like the hug, the jump, and the moment never happened.

After giving my parents a rundown of my horrendous day, I texted Meg. She said Bernie seems all right and promised to see her doctor first thing in the morning.

Sam, it's not your fault,

Meg texted.

Don't worry. ☺

How can I not worry? First I made the awful obit mix up, then I nearly sent Bernie to the emergency room. I'm no longer worried about Harry yelling at me. I'm worried about him firing me.

It's practically midnight, and for hours now I've been fighting the urge to text AJ. To keep my mind occupied, I do some research on Bernie. Turns out, she's spent her entire career at the *Herald Tribune*; she even delivered the paper as a teenager. And Bernie actually wrote obits before working her way up and becoming a beat reporter. During her tenure, she covered municipal beats, the county courthouse, and the statehouse in Trenton, our capital city. She has won numerous awards for her reporting and served as city-desk editor before moving over to the copy desk as its chief. I feel bad for not knowing any of this sooner. What if something terrible had happened to her? Bernie has earned the right to call me Moronica.

In the morning, I'm up early. To be honest, I don't remember sleeping. I stay in bed and watch through my bedroom window while the horizon goes from black to pink and gray swirls as the sky gradually lightens. It's probably a good thing that I'm off today. The more space I put between me and the Bernie event, the better my chances are for returning to the newsroom. I certainly attracted more attention than the gas station eyebrow plucker. I know one thing: I'll never forget how to spell *Raleigh*.

I reach for *Waiting for Godot* and flip through the first few pages. The title really spoke to me at the bookstore, but it's been sitting on the floor next to my bed, unopened, since then. My SAT practice book is down there too, collecting carpet fuzz. My parents think I should take the test again this fall to improve my chances of getting into Columbia or NYU. I can't make them understand that I'm fine with a state university; I'd prefer it. Especially since I have no idea what I want to do. Journalism was on the short list, but my confidence has been shaken. I wish my stakeout had been more fruitful and I'd been able to help Michael. I wish I hadn't made Bernadette so angry. I stare at the dialogue in *Godot*. I'm not really sure where it's going, but there does indeed seem to be a lot of waiting going on. Frustrated—by Beckett and everything—I slam the play closed and finally get out of bed.

My parents try to make me feel better when I come downstairs at six, dressed for a run. They both took the day off. They're going away for the long weekend and wanted to get a head start on holiday traffic.

Mom, who happens to be both in a related business and protective of her only child, is appalled that Bernadette made that kind of a scene over a misspelled city.

"I mean, come on. That was completely unprofessional. Copy editing is the wrong career for that woman if she's going to let an honest mistake get to her," she says.

"Yeah," I say, momentarily bolstered. "I thought that's what copy editors were for, anyway."

"Well, yes. But if you think journalism is a career you'd

like to pursue, you really do need to work on your spelling and grammar. It wouldn't kill you," she says.

"Or anyone else, for that matter," Dad says.

"You crack yourself up, don't you?" Mom says.

"Why, yes, I do," he says.

I'm not ready to laugh about this. My brain feels fuzzy from worry and lack of sleep. I need to clear my head. "I'm going to work out," I say.

"Why don't you run outside today?" Mom offers. "It's not that humid right now."

I consider it for half a second but don't feel like messing with my routine. "I'll stick to the treadmill."

I wind up running only three miles. Usually, running puts me in a better mental state, but I can't find a groove this morning, and all my tunes are getting on my nerves. When I emerge into the coolness of the air-conditioned kitchen, I hear Gram in the living room. On my way to the shower, I see she's sitting in her chair in front of the TV with a can of tomato sauce in each hand, apparently doing biceps curls.

"Getting some exercise in, Gram?"

"This lady is great. She's got a whole routine that I can do while sitting down," she says.

Gram is watching CTV, our municipal access television station. And there is indeed a woman in her sixties, sitting in a chair and performing arm exercises with actual dumbbells as opposed to canned vegetables. I'm wondering if this produces any results. The woman is not even breaking a sweat. But Gram seems to be enjoying herself; she's

even wearing yoga pants and Dad's old JUST DO IT Nike
T-shirt.

"Good for you, Gram!"

"You're not the only one who likes to stay fit."

Gram also likes to take walks and occasionally uses the
treadmill. She's in great shape for an older gal.

"Are you ready for our big bachelorette weekend?" I ask.

"You bet."

In a few hours, my parents will be joining the mass
Fourth of July exodus to coastal regions, or as we say in New
Jersey, they're going down the shore. They'll be staying at
my Uncle Lou's beach house near Island Beach State Park.

The fourth is Monday, but lots of towns have events
planned all weekend, and Harry wanted some extra phone
coverage. AJ's working Saturday, I'm working Sunday, and
we're both on for Monday. If I still have a job, that is.

My phone rings as I'm on my way upstairs. I look at the
screen. I was expecting Shelby, but I'm pleased to see it's
Meg.

"Hey!" I say.

"Hey, kiddo. Listen, I know you have the day off, but
Harry wants you to ride around with me today. Michael's
still out, so I'm going over to East Passaic city hall," she says.
"Harry doesn't like to go two days in a row without someone
from the *Herald Tribune* popping in on our favorite mayor."

"Really? You mean, he doesn't want to fire me?" I ask.

"I told you last night, nobody blames you for what happened to Bernie. Her diet and work schedule finally caught

up with her. Harry says she's taking some time off. Probably a good thing. She needs to start thinking about retirement," Meg says. "Want me to pick you up and then we'll head over to city hall?"

"That would be great. Thank you," I say.

"See you soon."

My phone rings again. This time it *is* Shelby.

"So, we're on for the pool today?" she asks.

Oh, no. With all that's happened, I totally forgot.

"Shelby, I'm so sorry. I just got called in to work."

"I thought you had today off."

"I did. But Meg just called, and I've got to work."

"Fine. So, you'd rather work than hang out with me."

I don't want to offend Shelby, but she nailed it. Meg's call made me realize just how true it is. It's like they still want me on their team.

"Tell you what. My parents are going away, so why don't you sleep over tonight?" I offer as an attempt to keep the peace.

"Can we order pizza?"

"Sure."

"Fine. But you owe me a pool day."

"Tomorrow," I say, a plan forming in my head.

After the pool, we can take a walk to Bargain Books & Beans, where Shelby can fill out an application. It would be sweet to have someone on the inside to help me figure out what the deal is with Sy Goldberg. Plus, it would keep Shelby busy.

chapter eleven

Local News

It's close to lunchtime when Meg and I finally leave city hall. The intense midday day sun beats down, and heat rises from the pavement. Since summer began, I've been cocooned in air-conditioning and missing all this sunshine. Today's a perfect beach day, and suddenly, I'm longing for the last real summer Shelby keeps talking about—and seems to be partaking in herself—with nothing better to do than swim at the community pool or ride waves all day.

My longing is enhanced by the fact that our trip to city hall has been mind-numbingly boring. Is this the job I've been coveting?

"Michael and I both start our days in our towns, making rounds," Meg says as we walk along the sidewalk toward her car. "It's important to get face time with the people you cover. Build a rapport."

Today we visited the police and fire departments, the

health inspector's office, and the mayor's office, where we requested an agenda for next week's city council meeting and chatted with Mayor Amato, who, not surprisingly, is very charming and probably considered attractive for an older man.

"Why'd you pick up the agenda so far in advance?"

"To see if anything interesting is coming up for a vote. It helps to be able to make calls and do some research beforehand. Summer is usually a slow time of year for city government, but in the case of this mayor, Harry wants to make sure he knows we're keeping an eye on him."

"Gotcha."

As we drive back to the *Herald Tribune*, my stomach constricts at the thought of facing AJ. Should I act the same? Wait to see how he acts first? Bore him with a minute-by-minute account of my morning at city hall? I needn't have stressed about it. As soon as we get through the newsroom door, Harry summons me.

"D'Angelo!" he calls from the city desk, where he's standing up and paging through his stack of newspapers. "My office. Pronto."

Turns out, being scared breathless is a real icebreaker.

"Wish me luck," I say to AJ as I put my stuff down on the obit desk.

"If you're not out in fifteen minutes, or if I hear any furniture crashing, I'm coming in after you."

"My hero."

I skulk into Harry's office, notebook and pen in hand,

and sit down in a chair facing his desk. I haven't been in here since I interviewed with him in May, when I got my armadillo hand stamps and felt oddly pleased by this strange initiation. My eyes travel past the toy-filled desk to the bookcase behind him, and I see something I hadn't noticed then—an actual stuffed armadillo. Not a fluffy toy. Harry's peculiar.

"Do you know why I do this job, D'Angelo?" he asks after a couple of seconds' worth of silent staring, drawing my attention away from the leathery dead critter and back to Harry. "I'll give you a hint: It's not for the job security."

Even I know the future of print journalism in general does not look good, and the *Herald Tribune*'s situation is even more dire. Who knows if we'll even exist a year from now? I refrain from commenting on his comment, however, and tackle his first question.

"You love it?"

"I do," he says. "I come in here every day excited about what we'll find out. For me, newspapers are the art of the possible. Anything is possible when you *care*. Do you *care* about what you're doing, D'Angelo?"

"I'm really sorry about the mix-up and about *Raleigh*, Harry. I was having a bad—" I say, but Harry holds up his hand and cuts me off.

"Do you know why I have you take obits over the phone?" he asks.

"No, but I did wonder why funeral homes couldn't just

e-mail us their obits. Or fill out a form on the website or something."

What I thought was an innocent comment sets Harry off.

"I know it seems like everyone is tweeting, blogging, and social-networking themselves to death these days looking for their fifteen minutes with one-sentence witticisms, but around here, I'm looking to get things right. And my way forces my editorial assistants to be accurate. I'm trying to teach you something here," he says. "No one wants to piss off a family member. Or Bernie, for that matter."

"I found that out," I say.

Harry pauses, and I watch his blood red face fade to a more reasonable peachy color.

"It also teaches you how to do phoners—phone interviews," he says.

"I understand," I say.

"I don't think you do," he says. "I want you to be more accurate, but I also want you to start writing obits that show me you care. Especially the features. Your leads are boring and unimaginative."

"I try to stick to the format," I say.

"Forget the format. You're writing someone's life story," he says. "There's room for creativity on the obit page. I want you to start reading the obits in the *New York Times*. You should already be reading the *Times* every day. And the *Post* and the *Journal,* and whatever else you can get your hands on. I can teach you to be a reporter, but you have to read more to be a better writer. Of course, both of those points are moot until you decide you're ready to care about what you're doing."

I open my mouth to object, but Harry cuts me off.

"About what *you're* doing, D'Angelo. Not what Michael's doing. Let him take care of his own beat."

I *do* care about my job. I just find Michael's more interesting. Still, I want to redeem myself for the obit blunder, my lackluster leads, and whatever health crises I seem to have triggered in Bernie. But I say nothing. He's calming down now, and I don't want to set him off again.

"So, with that said, I've got two assignments for you."

"Article assignments?" I was hoping I could leave, since this is my day off and all, but I'm not going to push it.

"One is," he says. "First I want you to go around the office and collect two dollars from everyone and put it in an envelope. If anyone gives you trouble, tell them you're doing it for me and if they have a problem, they can come and talk to me about it."

"Okay." I'm guessing it's a collection for Bernie, but I'm not questioning Harry. "What's the second?"

"I want you to write a feature obit," he says. "Get started now so I can read it myself before I leave tonight. In fact, with Bernie on leave, I'll be reading *all* feature obits from now on."

"Shouldn't I ask AJ how many he's got so far?"

"I don't care how many we've got so far. Go over to

your desk and ask AJ to e-mail you the first obit that came in today. That's your feature."

"Bernie usually waits to see who's the most interesting."

His tone is sharp when he answers me. "Everybody has a story, D'Angelo. Today it's your job to find that person's story and write the best damn obit you've ever written. *And* you're going to shake down everyone in this room for two bucks. Got it?"

"Got it," I say. "I promise I'll try harder."

Harry grimaces. "Famous last words."

As I expected, AJ is confused when I ask him to e-mail me the first obit of the day.

"Why?" he asks.

"Because I'm supposed to write the feature on that person," I say.

"That doesn't make any sense. This woman was pretty average, sorry to say."

I'm bummed. I didn't think I'd be working a full day.

"I guess I should get started."

"Did Harry scream at you?" AJ asks gently.

"Scream? Not really. More like lectured. Loudly. He told me I've got to learn to be more accurate and to care about this job. Oh yeah, and he told me my leads are boring and unimaginative," I say.

"You're lucky. I made the same mistake once—got a name wrong. He came out of his office, called me a friggin' idiot in front of everyone, and walked away. Harry's not bound by rules of political correctness."

"Maybe he didn't scream at me in front of everyone because I'm a girl."

"Nah. It's because he likes you."

"You think so?"

"Not in a lecherous-old-guy way," he says. "Because you're a good writer."

"Yeah, right."

"Seriously."

I shrug my shoulders. "But maybe I'm not a good reporter."

I decide to get the call to the family over with first. I call the funeral home and ask them to put me in touch with the family. The director says he'll call back with their home number as soon as he has permission to give it out. I walk over to the supply closet, take out a manila envelope, and commence my second task of the day—the shake-down. I start with Jack, since he's the nicest person in the newsroom.

"Hi, Jack. Harry asked me to collect two dollars from everyone," I say.

"Sure," he says. He reaches for his wallet, pulls out two bucks, and forks it over without another word. Next up, his assistant, Fran Garcia.

"Hey, Fran. Harry asked me to collect two dollars from everyone," I say.

"Did he say what it was for?" she asks.

"Nope."

"Aren't you curious?"

"I'm in no position to ask questions," I say.

"Gotcha. Here you go," she says, handing me her money.

I work my way around the room, collecting money and writing names down on the outside of the envelope as I go along. The responses to my demand vary, but in the end, nearly everybody hands over the money. When I emerge from sports, I notice Tony has arrived. This would be a good time to take a bathroom break and fix my hair and makeup (more like apply makeup)—before talking to him. The bathroom mirror reveals that I look even plainer than I expected, and of course all I've got on me are mascara and lip balm. I'm swiping mascara on my lashes when Meg walks in.

"Hey there," she says, smiling at me in the mirror. "I hope Harry wasn't too hard on you. He wouldn't bother if he didn't see your potential."

"AJ said the same thing."

"Smart guy, that AJ."

I pull out my ponytail holder and brush the tangles out of my long, straight hair.

"You know," Meg says, "you've got some great reddish highlights in your hair. Have you ever thought about going with a really dramatic red?"

"You mean dye my hair? My mom is a redhead. Auburn, actually."

"See? It's in your genes. It would look pretty. Think about it. I've got a guy who does great color work. Jimmi Gerard. I can hook you up."

"Thanks," I say absently.

Meg enters a stall, leaving me to envision this *dramatic* red. I leave my hair down, apply some Blistex, and consider myself as ready as I'll ever be to talk to Tony when I emerge from the ladies' room. I drop my purse off at my desk and retrieve my collection envelope.

"Uh, Tony?"

"Yep?" he says, swiveling around and smiling. This guy is always smiling. My heart does a drumroll, complete with some high-hat-cymbal action.

"Harry asked me to collect two dollars from everyone in the newsroom," I say.

"Do you do everything Harry asks?"

"Pretty much."

"Lucky Harry," he says, and makes serious eye contact.

Part of me knows it's Tony being Tony, and part of me doesn't care. I know I'm blushing, but I pretend I haven't heard his comment. When he hands me the money, I swear he lets his hand linger slightly longer than necessary. It's possible I'm making stuff up now. Still, as I settle into my desk chair, it doesn't stop my brain from launching into a full-blown fantasy involving me, Mousy D'Angelo, walking into the senior prom with Tony. Just once I want to be that girl. Not the one who gets insulted by the popular girls at parties or triggers health crises in copy editors. I want to be the girl all the other girls want to be.

"I see you looking at him," AJ says.

"Who? What are you talking about?"

"Coma Boy."

"Please."

"But you were."

"Was not—okay, I'm ending this exchange right now. Besides, how do you know I was looking at him? Were you looking at me?"

The phone rings and saves AJ from coming up with some quick retort that would undoubtedly involve insulting the size of my head or something. It's the funeral director with the phone number for my feature obit.

"I have to say," the director offers, "her daughter was a bit confused by the request. Although I'm sure she was a very nice woman, basically she was a housewife. I'm not sure how much more they have to share."

"Hopefully, enough for me to write one good story," I say. "Thank you for the number."

I hang up with the funeral director and decide to hit the *New York Times* online obituaries for some inspiration. Harry told me that important and famous people already have an obit in the can at most major newspapers. All that's missing is the date of death. I don't know if that's flattering, depressing, or both. Among those with the prestigious honor of not only being on the *Times* obit page but being worthy of a feature, are an artist who hung out with Andy Warhol and once shot holes in one of his paintings with a pistol; the woman who invented sparkling water; a documentary cameraman who filmed the wreckage of the *Titanic*, and a superior-court judge. There are no housewives on the list. I take a deep breath and decide to get the call over with quickly.

"Hello, Mrs. Abraham? This is Samantha D'Angelo. I'm an obit writer at the *Herald Tribune*."

"Yes, yes, we've been expecting your call," she says, sounding almost cheerful. "My sister and two brothers are here. We've been sitting around the kitchen table trying to figure out what we're going to say to you."

I want to confide in this woman that I've been sitting here trying to come up with some questions I can ask her about her mother, but she sounds so upbeat about the possibility of an interview that I don't have the heart to take this less than seriously.

"So, there are four siblings total? Two boys and two girls?" I ask.

"Yes, and eight grandchildren," she says.

"Growing up, did any of you play sports?"

"We all did. My sister played soccer, I played softball, my oldest brother was a football player, and our youngest brother was on the basketball team."

"Wow, your mother must have spent a lot of hours sitting in bleachers or on the sidelines. Or wasn't she a sports fan?"

"She wasn't that into sports when she married our father, but she learned all the rules of our respective games and even played a little. Hey, Alan, remember when Mom won the free-throw contest at your junior-varsity fundraiser? It was so funny. She threw ten granny buckets in a row and won a pizza party at Mario's. Of course she wound up taking the whole team. She was our biggest fan."

"That's very sweet," I say, a lead already forming in my head.

At the end of the call, Eileen Abraham thanks me profusely for giving her and her family a chance to sit around and remember happy times with their mother. It was nice to hear them all laughing and talking over each other during the interview.

I type my first paragraph.

> To her four athletic children, Abigail Kraus was more than just a loving, supportive mother—she was a mom for all seasons. Football and soccer in the fall, basketball in the winter, and softball in the spring. "She was our biggest fan," Eileen Abraham (née Kraus), her oldest daughter, said.

"It's a little Hallmark for my taste," Harry says later that day after he reads my story. "But it's a step in the right direction, D'Angelo. We'll try this exercise again and see what we get."

Again? Somehow, I thought this was a one-shot deal. How many more of these will I have to endure? I'm thankful Harry isn't going to make me rewrite this feature obit, but upset that it's going to take more than that to prove myself. I want to get back to important stuff.

"Oh, and D'Angelo?"

"Yeah."

"Send Bernie a fruit basket with the money you collected. She needs to eat better."

So much for investigative journalism.

chapter twelve

Jobs

Bargain Books & Beans is a lot more happening since my visit with AJ. They've set up a sidewalk café, and the wrought-iron tables are all occupied by parents with kids in strollers and couples sipping iced coffee. It's Saturday, and Chestnutville is holding its pre–Fourth of July festival today, complete with blow-up bouncy things, face painting, and free concerts. No doubt the extra foot traffic downtown is good for business.

As promised, I spent most of the day with Shelby at the pool, and somehow convinced her to take a late-afternoon walk to the mayor's coffee shop so she could help me with snooping. Harry didn't say I couldn't help Michael on my own time.

Inside the coffee shop/bookstore, there're a few adults with laptops, and I recognize a group of girls from our high school in the back. So does Shelby.

"Holy crap, Joanne Feinstein looks like she's lost about three hundred pounds," Shelby whispers in my ear.

Ignoring Shelby's hyperbole, I look toward their table. Wow. She looks fantastic. Fiona Baxter is behind the counter. She's the editor of our high school's literary magazine, *Folio*. With a name like Fiona Baxter, could she be anything else? Fiona is friends with Joanne, the yearbook editor, and the other girls at Joanne's table; all of them write for *Folio*, the yearbook, or both. I walk up to the counter with Shelby.

"Hey, Fiona," I say.

"Hey, Sam!" She's one of those perpetually upbeat people who can be superannoying sometimes. But I've never heard her utter a nasty word about anyone, so she gets points for being genuine.

"How long have you been working here?"

"This is my second week."

"Are they still hiring?"

"Why? You need a job?"

"Not me. Shelby." I touch Shelby's elbow and guide her toward the counter. "I've been working for the *Herald Tribune* this summer."

"Cool. Writing stories?"

"Kinda. Obituaries mostly."

"Really?" Joanne says.

Shelby pipes up. "I know, right? Who knew people wrote those."

"I'm hoping to do more news, though." I try to say it without sounding like I'm bragging.

"Nice. Well, if you want to write for *Folio* this year, just let me know."

"Thanks. I will."

"Anyway," Fiona says, "I don't know if we're hiring, but Shelby can fill out an application. Let me see if I can find one."

Fiona retreats through a swinging door, presumably to some kind of kitchen/office. Shelby's scanning the place, looking at all the used books and magazines. "I honestly don't think I want to work here, Sam. I need a place with an employee discount I can *use*."

"Shh. I'm just hoping you get called for an interview. Then you can ask a few questions. Help me find out what the deal is."

"What kind of questions?"

On the walk here, I tried my best to break it down for Shelby and explain what the *Herald Tribune* has been looking into. How Michael thinks Sy Goldberg is collecting a city salary without doing any work and how he's a partner—a very silent partner—in Bargain Books & Beans.

"Well, maybe the mayor or Sy Goldberg will interview you. That would answer some questions right there. Maybe we can find out how often you get paid and who signs your checks."

"Why don't *you* apply, then?"

"Because you're the one who needs a job."

Fiona returns from the back room. "Here ya go. Just fill this out and I'll give it to the manager. Need a pen?"

Shelby wordlessly collects both the pen and the

application, and we walk to a table in the back, near Joanne Feinstein.

"Hi, Sam. Shelby," she says. Joanne is beaming, and I can tell she's proud of her new body. She should be! She hasn't lost the exaggerated three hundred pounds, but she's shed some significant weight and is no doubt wearing single-digit jeans.

"Joanne," Shelby says, "you look awesome."

"Gorgeous!" I agree.

Her pals just sit there, lost. They've all got that look on their face—the one that says, *Yeah, yeah, the fat girl got thin. Now what are the rest of us supposed to do?* I get it. Change is hard to accept. Sometimes our friends need us to be a certain way. I'm not sure what comes first, the needing or the being.

I try to make small talk while Shelby fills out the application.

"So, are you all doing yearbook this year?"

There's a chorus of "yeahs," and Joanne says, "You're welcome to help out if you've got a free period."

The job offers are pouring in. "Thanks. How's the Fourth of July fest going? Did you guys check it out?"

"Nah," says one of the girls, whose name I don't know. "But we'll be at the fireworks tomorrow. What about you?"

Shelby looks up from her application. "Fireworks! You're not working are you, Sam?"

"During the day. I should be free at night."

Shelby puts the finishing touches on her application, and we say our good-byes.

"See ya, Joanne, girls," I say.

"Bye, guys!" Joanne says.

We walk up to the counter, and Shelby hands Fiona her application.

"Hey, Fiona," she says. "Settle a bet for us. Sam says the manager probably signs the paychecks around here. I say it's the owner."

I'm floored. I seriously didn't think Shelby listened to a word I said.

"Looks like you win, Shelby! It's definitely the owner. Mr. Goldberg."

"It is? What's he look like?" I ask.

"I don't know," Fiona says. "I've never seen him. Mr. Amato usually drops off our paychecks. He's my manager's dad, you know."

"That's interesting," I say.

"Okay then, Fiona. Thanks for that," Shelby says. "Maybe we'll be working together soon."

I'm still recovering from both Shelby's initiative and what I've just learned. Seems like no one ever sees Sy Goldberg. He's like the Easter Bunny.

Shelby pulls my arm and drags me toward the door.

"I hear music. Let's see if the band's any good," she says.

"Thanks, Fiona," I call over my shoulder.

"Anytime. And, hey, Sam, remember what I said about writing for us."

When we step onto the sidewalk, Shelby looks at me and says, "And that's how you solve Blue's Clues."

No kidding. Who knew she had it in her?

We cross the street and walk toward the public library. The band is set up on the gazebo near the town duck pond. They're young—like, high school age—although I don't recognize any of them.

"They're not bad," I say as we draw nearer. "Kinda have a surf-rock thing going on."

"The lead singer looks cute, but I can't tell from here," Shelby says. "Come on, let's get closer."

We approach the crowd in front of the band. I scan the group to see if there's anyone we know. There's a cluster of girls toward the front singing along to every word. Group-ies or girlfriends, hard to say which. Hanging toward the back chatting are two men and two women I'm pegging as band parents, and off to the side, talking to a girl with short shorts and braids, is AJ. He's got a pen and reporter's note-book in his hand, so I'm guessing he got sent out to work on a holiday story. I'm about to say hi when the girl puts her hand on his upper arm and leans in close to his ear. My breath quickens. AJ grins and shakes his head as she talks. Reflexively, I grab Shelby, pull her around the side of the gazebo, and hide behind a bush.

"Ouch, Sam. What are you doing? I can't see."

"AJ's here."

Shelby takes a step away. "He is? Where?"

"Wait, no!" I scream, and reel her in.

"Why not? I wanna meet him."

"He's talking to some girl."

"So? What's the big deal?"

Did he come here with her, or is it someone he just met? He wouldn't take a girl along on a work assignment. I peer around the shrubbery, and Shelby nudges me out of the way.

"Lemme see."

"How would you know who he's—"

"Jessica Palladino."

"Wha . . . you know her?"

"She graduated from Chestnutville High two years ago. She's Jason Palladino's older sister."

I've got to hand it to Shelby. She knows a lot of people and floats between cliques easily without ever becoming part of one.

"Come on," Shelby says. "Let's go talk to them."

"No, Shelby, please. Let's go home. He's working. I don't want to bug him."

Shelby hesitates for a split second and then gives in. "Fine," she says. "Doesn't look like he's working. Looks like he's talking to a girl. But maybe that's what's really bothering you."

"Let's go." I walk toward the duck pond with Shelby following. With Jessica at his side and the gazebo in his line of sight, hopefully AJ didn't notice me.

chapter thirteen

Senior Connections

I'm not a big fan of the Fourth of July. It's like an anomaly in the time-space continuum. Technically, it comes at the beginning of the summer. But once the long holiday weekend passes, it feels like summer's half-over. It bums me out because I'm never in any rush to get back to school.

To make matters worse, I'm sitting on six feet of powder blue velour that is the back seat of Aunt Connie's cavernous Lincoln. Seventeen can't come fast enough.

"Are you sure you've got a ride home?" Gram asks.

"Positive." I'm not sure, but I'll risk it.

I'm getting carsick back here. Aunt Connie maneuvers a car like it's a boat, drifting left to right like we're on choppy waters. She seems oblivious to the fact that's she's in control of this vehicle.

"Where are you ladies headed?" I ask.

"We're getting manicures," Gram says.

"We're going to a wake tomorrow," Aunt Connie says.

As if one is a requirement for the other.

"You need to get your nails done for a viewing?" I ask.

"Of course. We'll be shaking the widower's hand," Gram says. "I'm getting a paraffin wrap so my hands are extra soft."

"It won't matter. I always get in line ahead of your grandmother," Aunt Connie says. "I usually wink at the widower."

"But I give his hand an extra squeeze," Gram says.

"Don't tell me you're frequenting wakes to pick up old men," I say.

Aunt Connie laughs. "It beats ShopRite."

Is there a name for cougars on Social Security?

Gram turns serious. "We're just having fun. My husband was my husband. And that was that."

Poor Gram. I regret teasing her. She shared her life with Gramps for more than fifty years. How do people find that kind of forever love? How do you keep going when that person is gone?

I need to be a better granddaughter and take Gram to a movie or something. I don't care how old she is—wakes should not be a source of entertainment. My thoughts are interrupted by an abrupt shift in the Lincoln. Aunt Connie is pulling up in front of the *Herald Tribune* and seems to be angling for the parking lot. I do not need her careening into anyone's car.

"You can drop me right here!" I say too sharply. "The street is fine."

Aunt Connie screeches to a halt at the curb. I made her nervous.

"Bye, hon," Gram says.

"Bye, Gram. Thanks, Aunt Connie." I lean over the front seat, give them each a quick kiss on the cheek, and hope no one sees me getting out of the car.

———

I hope today isn't so bad, I think as I cross the parking lot to the side entrance. Turns out working yesterday—a Sunday during a holiday weekend—was the worst. The hours passed by slowly, and with no one to talk to, I spent way too much time thinking about seeing AJ with *Jessica.* I liked it better when she was just a voice on the phone.

When I open the door, I'm thrilled to see Michael at his desk.

"Michael! You're back!" I almost give him a hug. And I'm so not a hugger. AJ's already here too, which makes me doubly happy Michael's back—he can act as a buffer.

"Sam-I-am," Michael says. The nickname is spreading. "What's the good word?"

AJ holds up a hand. "Please do not ask him about the kidney stones. He's been referring to one as his first child, Irving, all morning."

I cover my ears and start humming a nonsense song. "I'm not hearing this. I'm definitely not hearing this."

Michael laughs. "Follow any mayors lately?"

I shoot AJ a look. "You told him?"

"Irving? I had to change the subject," AJ says.

"Did AJ tell you about ending up at a bank three towns away? In Belleville?" I ask.

"Yep. Unless he robbed it, there's no crime there," Michael laughs. "Not one that we can prove, anyway."

"I've got more news too," I say.

Michael smiles and puts his chin in his hand. "Enlighten me."

"Sy Goldberg signs the paychecks at Bargain Books & Beans."

"How'd you find that out?" Michael asks. I can tell he's surprised.

I told him how I made Shelby apply for a job there and how she asked Fiona to settle a bet for us.

Now AJ's shocked. "Your ditzy friend? Really?"

"Really. Fiona says Mayor Amato drops off their checks and that she has never seen Sy."

"No one has. That's just the thing," Michael says. "We suspect other people of having bogus jobs in the city. But all of them at least *pretend* to do something. They show up from time to time. No one has ever seen Sy. That's why I'm targeting him. It's my best chance at proving some kind of abuse of funding or power."

"So, you think the whole Sy-is-on-his-deathbed thing is a cover?" I ask.

"Sy is probably healthy as a horse and collecting a paycheck in Miami," Michael says. "That's my best guess."

"You've done searches on him?" I ask.

"Of course. Nexis, Google, the works. Nothing turned up, which doesn't mean anything except that nothing's been written about him."

It's sad to think that for some people, an obit is the only time they'll be in print, and then they're not even around to enjoy it.

I survey the sparsely populated newsroom and throw *Waiting for Godot*, *CosmoGirl*, and *Seventeen* onto my desk. Only a handful of people are in, which is only slightly better than yesterday, when it was only Rocco and me. I raise my eyebrows when I see Tony's here. Alice too, which means Harry's in his office.

"I'm glad I brought some backup entertainment," I say.

"Yeah, a lot of people took the holiday off," Michael says. "Stinks to be the intern. Been there."

"Why are you here?" I ask Michael.

"Just trying to get caught up after—"

"Yeah, yeah. Irving, we know," AJ says. He's fiddling with the ring around his neck. I find the Jessica thing puzzling.

The door smacks open, and in walks photog Alexis. There goes my plan for quality face time with Tony. Michael and AJ watch her go by and exchange that *knowing* guy look. I don't blame them. It's hard not to. Her legs are nearly as long as my whole body. She looks like she belongs in front of a camera, not behind one.

What I wouldn't give to look like her for just one day.

Meg comes bounding through the door and walks toward the obit desk. "It's dead in here. No pun intended." Meg laughs. "This is the kind of day that requires an afternoon field trip to the megadrugstore and some bubble tea. Wanna come, Sam?"

"Sure. If Harry lets me leave," I say. "What's bubble tea?"

"You've never had it? You are so coming along. I'll talk to Harry," she says.

"Okay, then." I'm happy to have something to look forward to, since this seems like the start of another uneventful day.

I spend the morning answering a barrage of phone calls from people—clueless people who obviously can't read or Google—inquiring about the start times and locations for various parades, festivals, and fireworks. I also field a few complaint calls from older people who don't like the way our newspaper's ink gets all over their hands. Just like the obit versus death notice question, I get at least one of these calls a day. We apparently have substandard ink at the *Herald Tribune*. One more advantage to reading the news on smartphones, tablets, and laptops.

"Hey, Sam. I'm taking off."

I glance up to see Tony standing by my desk, and I quickly turn toward my computer screen and click on something, anything, so he doesn't see how nervous he makes me. AJ is sitting across from me, on the phone.

"Can you do me a favor? If this person calls, can you

have her call my cell?" He hands me a piece of paper, as if I've already said yes.

"I'm covering a concert in Liberty State Park tonight. She's supposed to hook me up with VIP parking."

"Sure, no problem," I say.

He begins to walk, stops midstride, and turns around. "If you don't have plans, I've got a plus one. You're welcome to come along."

Are you kidding me? I'm there! That's what inner Sam screams. Outwardly, it's business as usual. The responsible-to-a-fault people pleaser.

"Uh-oh. I can't. I've got plans to see the fireworks with a friend."

"Well, have fun," he says.

"You too."

"Hey, and don't forget. Bar night on Wednesday. We missed you last week."

AJ's off the phone now and listening, I can tell.

Holy crap! Did that just happen? I'm such an ass. An amazing-looking guy asks me to do something fun, and I totally blow him off. Why don't I just bag my evening with Shelby? It's my parents' fault for raising me to be so loyal. Maybe it's not too late. I look down at his number in my hand. I can give it a half hour and call his cell. My stomach gets all floaty at the thought, and then AJ pokes a hole in my happiness bubble.

"He's probably looking for help writing the review. It's some eighties act."

"Oh yeah! He said he missed me at bar night too. Did he want me to write a review of *that*?" I'm so pissed, I can barely keep my voice from shaking. "At least he asks me to do things. Not like some people who cover bands in my town and don't bother calling."

AJ looks temporarily perplexed but quickly gets on board. "Are you talking about that thing in Chesnutville on Saturday? I thought you'd have something better to do." Then he looks up over the top of his glasses. "How'd you know I was there, anyway?"

"It was in the paper! You wrote about it?" Thankfully, I remembered that small fact. "Speaking of which, don't you have a parade to cover?"

"I do indeed," he says.

"You'd better get out of here."

My mood takes a serious dive after AJ leaves. It doesn't help that Michael also packs up to go and I'm alone on my side of the newsroom. I do make myself smile, however, with the comical mental image of AJ at his parade, surrounded by kids with balloons, people waving flags, and marching Boy Scouts. He doesn't seem like the kind of guy who does anything in daylight.

I call Shelby around lunchtime to see if her mom can pick me up after work. I don't want to ask AJ today.

"Sure," she says. "We're still on for fireworks, right?"

"Of course," I say, trying to sound happy about it.

Meg rescues me around one o'clock. I've been flipping through *Seventeen*. I can't believe their back-to-school issue is out already. Oh where, oh where is this fictional high school from the *Seventeen* magazine photo shoot with girls sporting the latest fall fashions as they walk toward the front doors of their school, leaves scattered at their feet, a perfect mixture of warm autumnal colors? Disgusted, I toss the magazine aside. I've had enough false hope for one day.

"Whatcha doing?" Meg asks.

"I just took a quiz called 'Do You Take Enough Beauty Risks.'" I tell Meg. "I don't."

"What counts as a beauty risk? Applying lipstick while driving on the New Jersey Turnpike? Getting a bikini wax from an unlicensed technician?"

Meg has porcelain skin, big, blue eyes and straight black hair she wears in a perfect, chin-length bob. Although she's probably considered curvy by high school standards, in the real world, it doesn't seem to matter. The men in the news-room are always checking her out—just like they do Alexis—the difference being that Meg is genuine.

"Still going to the drugstore?" I ask. "I'm feeling a strange urge to buy berry lip gloss and navy mascara."

"Sounds like a plan," she says. "Let's go."

It's more than an hour later when Meg and I finally walk into the newsroom with our haul from the drugstore and bubble tea (I got mango; it's delicious). I'm beginning to panic about being gone so long, but Harry doesn't yell at me or anything. I'm sure the burger Meg brought back for him helped.

I see AJ is at his computer, working on his parade story,

no doubt. We work in silence for a while before AJ gets up, wanders over to the TV, and starts flipping through channels. When he lets out a really loud yawn, I look up from my computer to see him stretching his arms and twisting his back like he's warming up for a run. His shirt is more formfitting than usual, and I find myself staring at his broad back and biceps. Drummer muscles, I guess. My skin feels warm and tingly. I quickly look at my screen again when he turns around and starts heading back toward his desk.

"Still mad at me?" AJ asks.

"I wasn't mad."

"Good. 'Cause I was only pointing out the obvious about Coma Boy," he says.

"What? That he uses people? Sounds an awful lot like dating some girl and then referring to her as your I-don't-know."

My annoyance resurges as I picture AJ with Jessica on Saturday and the way he was absently touching the ring around his neck this morning.

"Are you talking about Jessica? Because I never said—"

I cut him off. "You don't have to tell me. I don't want to know. Who you date is your own business."

AJ opens his mouth to say something but perhaps thinks better of it.

We drift back into another forty-five minutes of working without talking, till my ride arrives and I can finally put my superslow Fourth of July weekend at the *Herald Tri-bune* to bed. Seems like even death took a holiday.

"Nice job on that parade story," Harry says to AJ as quitting time approaches. "I hate parades, but your writing convinced me that this one was worth seeing."

"Thanks," AJ says.

It must have been some article, because Harry's in an exceptionally good mood and doesn't make either of us write a feature obit. Maybe he has a barbecue to get to.

chapter fourteen

Holiday Wrap-Up

Shelby's mom drops us both off at my house after work. The plan is to have pizza with Gram and then walk downtown for the annual prefireworks reunion. It's been only a few weeks since we've seen our classmates, and yet we all flock to Memorial Field, the high school's football stadium, to walk laps around the bleachers and check one another out.

"You're sure you don't want to come with us, Gram?" I feel guilty leaving her home by herself again. I haven't been around that much this weekend.

"You two have fun. You don't need an old lady like me tagging along."

"You're not old," Shelby says. She loves Gram. "You should see Ms. Highland, the eleventh-grade English teacher. Now, *she's* old. She's, like, too senile to even be teaching. Sometimes her wig shifts when she's writing on the chalkboard."

Gram reaches absently toward her wavy gray hair that she keeps stylishly short. "I'm glad I inherited my father's good locks."

The doorbell rings. My grandmother hands me some money.

"Pay for the pie, hon," Gram says. "Maybe it's a cute boy."

I peek through the skinny window alongside the door to see if it's anyone we know. He's not cute as Gram had hoped. He's not even a boy. He is old. Not old like my parents, old like Gram.

"Uh, Gram. I'll let you handle this one," I say. I walk back into the kitchen and hand her the money.

Gram returns a few minutes later carrying the pizza.

"Would you believe that was Freddy from the senior club?" Gram says. She puts the pizza on the kitchen table.

"*Freddy*, huh?" Shelby teases.

Grandma actually smiles and waves Shelby off in an aw-shucks kind of way. Great. Now my grandmother is getting more action than I am. I reach for a slice of pizza and take a bite.

"So, what are you going to do tonight?" Shelby asks.

"Watch the New York City fireworks on TV like I always do."

"You should have gone to the family picnic, Gram. You could have watched the fireworks on the boardwalk," I say.

"Are you kidding me? I'm not going to any family functions until that witch Angie apologizes."

The D'Angelos are notorious grudge holders. There is always some cousin or aunt or uncle who's at odds—or full-out warring—with another family member. The Gram–Aunt Angie feud is a fairly recent one (some last for years) and concerns Aunt Angie's oldest son, the podiatrist. Gram made the mistake of patronizing a local foot doctor instead of having someone drive her the seventy-five miles to Aunt Angie's son's office in Toms River to have what amounted to nothing more than a high-tech toenail clipping. One has to wonder how word of Grandma's toenail clipping ever got out. Not that it matters. Our family arguments are rarely grounded in logic.

Still, I know Gram is just using this as an excuse. She probably wanted to give my parents some space.

"You girls get ready to go," Gram says when we're finished eating. "I'll wrap up the rest of the pizza."

"Thanks, Gram," I say.

"Come on, Sam," Shelby says. "I can touch up my makeup while you change."

"What's wrong with what I've got on?"

Shelby is wearing a star-spangled ensemble, complete with a red-white-and-blue halter. I was planning on wearing the same jeans and T-shirt I've had on all day.

Shelby rolls her eyes at my grandmother. "Upstairs. Let's go," she says.

In my room, Shelby reapplies her red lipstick while I look through my closet. She looks at me in the mirror.

"Why don't you wear that miniskirt? Show off your runner's legs."

"My legs are fat," I say.

"Would you stop? You're a size four," she says. "Your legs are athletic."

"I want them to be skinny," I say.

"Just shut up already," she says, and joins me at my closet.

She makes me change into a denim miniskirt and red tank top with skinny straps—and apply lip gloss—before we make the one-mile trek downtown.

———

After one lap around Memorial Field, Shelby runs into Mark, the guy behind the keg at the island-themed pool party. Mark is flanked by two guys, one of whom is that Josh guy who wanted me to play Quarters.

"Hi, Shelby," Mark says. "Where ya been? I've missed you."

"Around," she says.

"Wanna sit with us?"

Josh stares at me like he's trying to make me look at him. I chew on my lower lip.

"Maybe," she says. "We're walking right now."

"We'll be under the scoreboard if you want to come and look for us."

"Okay," Shelby says.

When they're out of earshot, Shelby whips her head at me. "Why do you do that?"

"Do what?"

"Nothing. That's the problem. Cute guys want to sit with us, and you don't even talk to them."

"You mean cute guys want to sit with *you*, and besides, that guy Josh was mean to me."

"Mean? How? When?"

I tell her about how he called me Angry Girl when I didn't want to play Quarters with him.

"Did you ever think maybe he was flirting and you blew him off? You can be sort of . . . stuck-up sometimes."

"Stuck-up? Where'd you get that? I'm shy."

"I know that, Sam. But not everyone does. *Shy* can come off as snobby. It puts people off. Like Nick Costas. I know he liked you. He always stared at you when you were at your locker."

Is that true? It can't be. "If he liked me, why didn't he ask me out?"

"He was probably afraid of getting shot down. Like I said, you can be—"

"Stuck-up. Yeah, I heard you."

"I'm trying to help. You scare guys."

"Scare guys? What? No, I don't."

I consider what Shelby said as we meander toward the permanent, concrete bleachers and look around for a place to sit. We find some space toward the top and climb the stairs. Once we settle in, I decide to tell Shelby what happened with Tony today. I want to get her take, but more important, I need to prove that some guys aren't afraid of me.

"There's this amazing-looking guy at work."

"AJ?"

"What? No. Not AJ. Why would you say that?"

"Hellooo. The shrubbery? Jessica Palladino?"

I get queasy when I think about it. I shake my head.

"Forget AJ. I'm talking about Tony."

"Oh, okay, Tony," Shelby says. "And . . ."

I relay my brief Tony encounters for her—the flirta-tious body contact, the walk to the deli, the concert invite—but I keep the bar-night information to myself. If Shelby knew that such an opportunity existed, she would bug me relentlessly to go.

"So. Whataya think?"

"He sounds like a total flirt, and don't forget, he *is* older," Shelby says. "But who cares? You should go for it."

"AJ thinks he uses people."

"So? You can use him. It would be good practice," Shelby says. "A perfect summer thing."

———

By Wednesday, I'm already regretting my decision to tell Shelby about Tony. Ever since I mentioned him at the fireworks on Monday, she's become my self-appointed love coach. Today I barely have time to plop my butt in my desk chair before the obit phone starts ringing. I know it's Shelby. I ignored the text she sent five minute ago. *Is TG in?* Henceforth, according to Shelby's instructions, Tony Roma is known as TG, for "the God."

"Obit desk," I say.

"Well?" I was right.

"Well what?"

"Is he there?"

"Not yet."

"Text me when he gets there."

"Why?"

"Sam, face it. If you want to get this guy, you're going to need my help."

"Hmm. Maybe I'll call Fiona this morning."

"Why?"

"Because if you're going to get a job this summer, you're going to need *my* help."

Talk of employment always gets Shelby off the phone. I should've kept my crush a secret. It always seems possible when it's all in my head. It's like Jane Eyre pining away for Mr. Rochester is almost better than when they finally get together.

My phone rings again. Where's AJ? Why must he always be late? I pick up the avocado-colored receiver. The decor at the *Herald Tribune* is so retro, I'm considering taking some of this stuff to the *Antiques Roadshow*, beginning with this phone.

"Obit desk."

"Samantha?" says a vaguely familiar voice. "It's Eileen Abraham, Abigail Kraus's daughter. I just wanted to thank you for the wonderful story you wrote about our mom. We could tell you really cared, and it meant a lot to me, my sister, and my brothers. I cut it out, and I'm going to have it laminated."

"You're welcome," I say. "It was a pleasure to write."

"You've got real talent, dear," she says.

"Thank you."

"What was that all about, D'Angelo?" Harry asks from behind me after I've hung up.

"Oh, just the daughter of the woman I wrote the feature about a couple of days ago. She wanted to thank me for the story."

"Imagine that," he says. "People actually care about obits."

"It was nice of her to—are you wearing a tie?"

My question makes his shoulders slump. "Meeting with the publisher today. Again."

"Is that bad?"

"Enjoy it while it lasts, D'Angelo."

"What?"

"Everything. Now get back to being an intern. That includes our feature-obit writing exercise. That should make your partner in crime here happy." Harry nods toward the arriving AJ when he says that last part.

"What's he talking about?" AJ asks.

I tell him about Eileen Abraham and how that seemed to remind Harry that I'm now the go-to girl for feature obits.

"That was a good story," AJ says. He's not wearing his glasses today. His eyes are a coppery shade of brown. He hesitates, then adds, "Reminded me of my mom."

"It did?"

"She used to go to all my swim meets."

"Wait. You swim?"

"Used to. Practiced every morning before school. In the winter, my mom was out in the driveway by five warming up the car."

The memory takes AJ somewhere else.

"Why'd you stop?"

"Swimming was something I did with my mom. When I lost her, I didn't care about swim meets anymore. There was nothing worth winning."

Poor AJ. My mom is such a constant presence in my life, sometimes I don't know how I feel about something until I gauge her reaction. I may not be able to talk about everything with her, but just having her there all the time is what makes things real.

AJ adjusts the ring around his neck, and suddenly I get it.

"So, drums?"

"Drums. I switched my effort into becoming the next Neil Peart. That's—"

"The drummer for Rush. I know," I say. "My dad—"

"Plays bass in an eighties cover band. We *all* know."

"I'd like to see your band sometime," I say.

"We're not playing out again until the Friday before Labor Day."

My eyes fall to the ring on its leather cord. I almost reach for it, but he tucks it into his shirt without looking at me. "What do you think? Bar night tonight. You in?"

"Seriously?" I say.

He rolls his eyes at me. It's nice to have sardonic AJ back. It was hard to watch his face when he was talking about his mom.

"I'm there!" I say.

The phone rings, and I pick it up.

"Obit desk?" I recognize the voice, and the smile leaves my face. "Sure, Jessica, he's right here. Hold on."

I hand the receiver to AJ. "I'm going to see if the mail's here," I say. He can talk to his *girlfriend* alone.

About a half hour later, I'm back at my desk when Michael crashes through the back door, his face the color of a pomegranate. I hope he's feeling okay. Do kidney stones come back?

"What are you doing here before lunch?" AJ asks.

"Got thrown out of city hall this morning."

"By the mayor?"

"Who else?"

"Can he do that?"

"Nope. He can't keep a list of all city employees *with* their salary histories from me either, but that's what he's been doing. He also refused to disclose the names of anyone who received aid from the weatherization board Sy is supposedly managing. The mayor'll be hearing from our lawyer again today."

"No more Mr. Nice Guy?" AJ asks.

"No more Mr. Nice Guy."

"Want us to follow him again?" I ask.

"Follow who, D'Angelo?" Harry booms from behind me. He's quite stealthy.

"Uh, no one," I say.

"That's what I thought. How's my feature obit coming?"

"Great!" I say, and look at my screen until Harry retreats to the city desk.

Around three o'clock, I take a break to watch part of the Mets-Phillies doubleheader. The TV is suspended from the ceiling at the far end of the city desk, above Rocco's head. Normally we're tuned in to some kind of news programming, but Harry is a huge Phillies fan and there is no shortage of Mets fans (i.e., gluttons for punishment) in the room, myself included. So an exception has been made. Tony and some of the guys from sports are gathered under the screen, heads tilted upward. Usually they're back in the sports department, listening to games on the radio or watching them on the Internet or the miniscule TV they have back there.

I'm sitting next to Rocco on his desk. The starting pitcher for the Mets is on the mound. There's a man on first, one out. The pitcher keeps throwing to first to keep the runner from stealing. He winds up and then quickly throws to first again.

"Balk!" I scream, unaware I had spoken aloud. It's how we watch baseball at our house. "Take your base!"

The guys turn around, amazed I got the call right even before the announcers. Tony smiles.

"All this and she knows baseball too," Tony says. His blue eyes lock on mine and linger there for a second.

Here come my nervous splotches. I'm too frazzled to focus on the game. I retreat to my desk to allow my body temperature to return to normal. Time to get crackin' on my feature obit, anyway. I'm about to start in on my lead when I hear Tony say, "Come on, Sam, I'll drive you to get coffee."

I wasn't planning on a coffee run at that very second. In fact, Harry is waiting for my feature obit. But then I think about the phone call from Jessica right after AJ invited me to bar night, and I can't help myself.

"Okay," I say, rising from my seat. "Just let me see who needs what."

———

Today, Tony has the top down on his black Mustang. All I keep thinking as we drive along Main Street is, *Please, God, please let someone from my high school see me with this guy, in this car!* Apparently I measure myself against the popular kids at Chestnutville High School, even when I'm not around them. They're like my constant Greek chorus.

"So, you're a big baseball fan, huh?" Tony asks.

"Yup. Mets," I say.

"Yankees," he says.

"Figures," I say.

"What's that supposed to mean?" he says, a smile in his voice.

"You just seem like a Yankee fan. Mets fans? It's like we don't expect to win. We're odd."

"Not odd," Tony says. "Pretty great if you ask me."

"Thanks," I say, keeping it simple and just accepting the compliment like they say to do in all those women's magazines, but about to freak inside.

The trip through the Dunkin' Donuts drive-through is a quick one, and Tony opens the car door for me when we get back to the newsroom.

"Let me take that," he says, reaching for the tray of coffees I've been balancing on my lap.

I return the favor and open the side door for him when we reach the building. As soon as I walk back into the newsroom, AJ looks at me quizzically when he sees me with Tony, who's carrying coffees. I offer no explanation—much like he never offers one about Jessica—as I finally settle in to put the finishing touches on my story. As soon as my hands hit the keyboard, my phone rattles. A text from Shelby. It's like she senses I've got work to do.

Party@Rob's. You in?

I text back.

Can't. Workin' late.

I get a return text seconds later.

☹

I wonder if she'll go to the party without me. I hope so. It will make me feel less guilty for not mentioning bar night.

After another long day in the realm of the unliving, I head to the ladies' room to primp for the Harp & Bard. I apply mascara and do the best I can with this liquid eyeliner I bought. I gloss my lips a coppery color, then brush out my hair and leave it long. I'm all set.

"Ready to go?" I ask AJ when I return.

"You mean you're not getting a ride from Coma Boy?"

I want to pinch him really hard, but instead I ignore him as I text my mom to tell her I'll be extra late and AJ will be taking me home. Another lie of omission. It feel tons worse, though, when it's my mom I'm hiding the truth from. This is so not me. I hesitate for a second and consider calling her to come clean, but then I skip it. It's not like I'm doing anything wrong, and anyway, how would she ever find out?

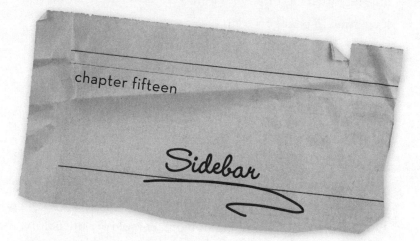

chapter fifteen

Sidebar

The Harp & Bard, despite its poetic name, is the kind of corner bar frequented by old men—three or four total on a *good* night—who come in, flop their ample butts down on the red vinyl barstools, and wait for the lottery on the lone television, which isn't even a flat screen. It's also the kind of bar that serves minors if they happen to be with the usual crowd from the *Herald Tribune*.

Most of the *Herald Tribune* people stand near the bar. The rest are at tables that look like they belong more in a seafood restaurant than a place that serves alcohol, stale pretzels, and very salty popcorn—which I begin absently munching on as I scan the room for Tony. I'm about to reach for another handful of sodium when, out of nowhere, a Bud bottle is presented to me from behind. I grab it and turn around to find Tony. It's like my heart fills with helium. He looks and smells nice. His hair has some gel in it, and he's wearing different clothes. I guess features interns have time to change.

"Thanks," I say.

"Cheers," he says, and clinks the top of my bottle.

Not wanting to embarrass myself, I put the bottle to my lips just as AJ is turning around.

"What're you doing?" he says.

"Lighten up, AJ. It's one beer," Tony says.

"She doesn't drink," AJ says.

Following through on the sip would feel disloyal to AJ. But not drinking will make me look completely uncool in front of Tony. I feel like an amateur actress in one of those corny DVDs about peer pressure we watched in junior high health class. I'm still trying to decide what to do when Harry puts an end to my internal struggle.

"Hand it over, D'Angelo," he says, putting his arm between me and Tony.

I comply without turning around to make eye contact. Harry has that effect on me.

He passes my beer to the nearest reporter, who shrugs and takes a swig as Harry walks back to his table of *Herald Tribune* people and sits down between Michael and Meg. AJ looks relieved, and I don't think Tony will try to buy me another round.

"I'm going to check out the jukebox," AJ says, and walks away.

Tony ignores the whole exchange and resumes talking to me as if nothing transpired.

"How old are you, anyway?" he asks.

"Seventeen," I say. "Next month."

"Really? I always assumed you were a college intern like me and AJ," Tony says.

"I'm going into my senior year in high school," I say.

"You look older," he says, smiling in a way that convinces me older is good. "Did you take your SAT yet?"

"Twice. I can take it again this fall, but then they average all three scores," I say. "It's not worth it unless I really need to."

"*Do* you?" he asks.

"I'm pretty sure I did well enough to get into my first choice," I say.

"Which is?" he asks.

"Penn State," I say. "For now."

Dad's alma mater. The D'Angelos are also big college football fans. (Mom went to Rutgers.) My parents have been taking me to see Penn State play since I was eleven. I like the familiarity of it.

"Good school. Just a little far, isn't it?" he asks.

"From what?" I ask.

"Civilization."

"Four hours from here," I say. "Not so bad."

Why would he care if I were going to college far away? He hardly knows me. Does he want to know me better? My mind starts making huge leaps.

"D'Angelo!" My name being shouted from clear across the room snaps me out of it. Meg is waving me over to an empty seat next to her.

"I'll be right back," I tell Tony, and make my way over

to Meg. She pulls out the chair and smacks the seat when I arrive.

"Sit down. Have a diet soda," she says, smiling.

"Or an apple juice," Harry says.

I sit down and look back and forth between her and Harry.

"Did you need me for something?"

"Just surprised to see you fraternizing with the competition." Meg says.

"Huh?"

"Coma Boy," she says, taking a sip of her beer, "wants to fill in for Michael in August."

That confirms what I thought, but I'm kinda shocked to hear Meg call him Coma Boy.

"Why does everyone call him that?" I ask.

"Because he stinks," Harry proclaims. "Because someone in a coma can write a feature story better than him. Coma Boy's just lucky his daddy and our *publisher* are old frat buddies, or I would have put AJ in that spot months ago."

From the way he says it, sounds like Harry's contempt for Tony and for our publisher is about equal. The *Herald Tribune* really is an alternate universe. Where else could the best-looking guy in the room become the object of ridicule because, in the words of our illustrious editor in chief, "he stinks"?

"Please do me a favor, D'Angelo," Harry says. "Don't stay in this business if you're just going to stink. It's not the kind of job you can do half-assed."

It's like being in a sea of bobblehead dolls, as nods of agreement make their way around the table like the wave. In addition to Harry, Meg, and Michael, the long table is also populated by Grace and Brian, the city-desk editors; Jim, the sports editor; and Jack. Make that bobblehead dolls amid a forest of empty brown bottles. These people can drink. I'm like the kid at the big-people's table on Thanksgiving. The *drunk*-big-people's table. I want to ask Michael what's going on with Sy Goldberg and the mayor, but it's clear Harry is holding court.

"Who am I kidding? We're all like a bunch of dinosaurs walking around with the comet speeding toward us, anyway," Harry says. "Enjoy working for a newspaper while you can, D'Angelo. Eventually, we're all going to be replaced by outsourcing. Some guy in Bangladesh is going to be writing your feature obits for $7.50 a pop. Provided there are any newspapers left."

The *Herald Tribune* is the media's version of the Brachiosaurus, plodding along like a 150-million-year-old lizard. While larger papers are talking about becoming completely web based, and publications specifically designed for handheld devices are being developed, we're still printing our paper the old way, and our website is, well, lame. I wonder if Harry had another long conversation with the publisher today. Changes are coming for the *Herald Tribune*, and clearly it's giving Harry agita.

I glance over my shoulder and see Tony at the bar talking to Alexis. I want to get away but can't. The more they drink, the more unsolicited advice I get.

"Take Spanish, if you haven't already," Grace says.

"Think about majoring in political science," Michael says.

"Don't just study writing, study everything you can," Jack says. "Good reporters are more like jacks of all trades and masters of none. You know, the type of people who make excellent *Jeopardy!* contestants."

And then there's Harry, who's becoming more interested in talking about himself than about the state of the news industry. AJ joins us halfway through Harry's war story—a real war story. Harry is telling us about a boy he met while covering the war in Bosnia for the *Christian Science Monitor.*

I learn a lot about Harry. The most obvious of which is that not only can Harry outwrite everyone in the newsroom, he can also outdrink them, for a while at least.

Meg comes back to the table with another round, and then Harry's stories *really* come out. I get the impression, however, that for everyone else at the table, this isn't exactly new material. Me, I'm riveted. Harry was captured by Bosnian Serbs after he discovered a mass grave of Muslim civilians. He was released two days later, after the UN packed on the pressure. Everyone thought he was going to win the Pulitzer for international reporting. But it didn't happen.

"Who gives a rat's ass about the Pulitzer?" he slurs.

"I'll bet Stephen King has often said that very same thing," says Jack, trying hard to lighten the moment. "I mean, sure, he writes horror, but what about the book about JFK and *Hearts in Atlantis*?"

"Are we talking about Atlantis the lost city or the hotel casino in the Bahamas?" Brian interjects out of nowhere. He's just as tanked as Harry, but he's been quieter about it until now.

"We were talking about the Pulitzer," Harry says, slapping the table with his open palm and spilling his beer, some of which travels across the table and into my lap before I have a chance to dodge it. "It's no wonder Bernie thinks you're all a bunch of morons."

At that point, Meg gently rests her hand on his arm, in a way I would have been afraid to. "Come on, boss, let's get Jack to drive you home," she says, and shoots Jack a look.

Suddenly, it's like there're two minutes left to the football game and Meg just called the hurry-up offense. Jack finishes his beer and pushes his chair away from the table.

"My wife is going to be calling me any second," Jack says. "Let's go, Harry. You're on my way."

Harry has a distant, angry look in his eyes, like a caged gorilla. The image is only enhanced by the fact that Harry is, well, hairy. Meg helps Harry out of his seat, and he walks wordlessly toward the door.

"Do you have a ride home, Sam?" she asks.

"Got it covered," AJ answers.

"See you tomorrow," she says, and then turns to follow Harry to the door.

Jack is quick to leave as well.

"Good night, everyone," Jack says. "Drive safe."

A chorus of "'Night, Jack," is followed by the sound of chairs scraping across the old linoleum floor. The huddle is broken as everyone makes a move for the exit. Grace and Brian take a last sip of their drinks and say their good nights. That leaves me, AJ, and the sports guy Jim.

"We're gonna take off too," AJ says. "See you to-morrow."

"Sure thing," Jim says.

"Well, that was fun," AJ remarks when we get up from the table. "Tonight I got to see a drunk, angrier Harry. Sweet."

I know AJ came tonight because of me and he didn't have any fun. But me, I can't wait for my next bar night. I'm at home in the land of misfit bobblehead dolls.

"I'm gonna hit the men's room," he says.

While I'm standing at the front door waiting for AJ, I feel a hand on either shoulder, neck-massage style. I turn to find myself face-to-face with Tony.

"I'm glad to see you made it out tonight, Sam."

"I had fun," I say.

"Good," he says.

He seems a bit buzzed. He's staring at me and saying something with that grin of his, something I'm supposed to understand.

"Too bad you couldn't make it to the concert Monday night. I'm covering the Journey/Foreigner tour at the end of the month. Maybe you can be my plus one for that?"

The door swings open, and Alexis pops her head in before I have a chance to answer.

"Tony! Are you coming?" She never glances my way or attempts to hide her impatience.

"Yeah, just a sec. We're going to another bar. Wanna come?"

"I can't," I began, "I'm . . ."

"Right. Keep forgetting." There's no hint of sarcasm in his voice. "Well, see you tomorrow."

"Sure." I can't say much more with Alexis continuing to glare at Tony and refusing to shut the door. Thankfully, AJ arrives after they leave so he doesn't witness my brief encounter.

"Let's hit it," he says, and opens the door for me.

Rocco walks in just as we're walking out.

"What up, man?" AJ says.

"Guess I'm late to the party."

"Harry reached his limit," I offer.

Rocco nods knowingly. "May as well grab a beer anyway." Rocco is heading for the bar when he turns around and says, "Oh, Sam. Your mom just called the newsroom. I told her you'd already left for the Harp."

"Uh, thanks." What I mean is, *Oh, shit!* I dig my phone out of my purse. Sure enough, there are three missed calls from her. I should have known better.

AJ arches his eyebrows at me. "Sam-I-am. Taking a walk on the wild side. And wearing makeup too. What's up with that?"

As we walk to AJ's car, my mind is reeling with thoughts of Tony. He says he was happy to see me out tonight, he squeezed my shoulders, he wanted me to go to Journey/Foreigner *and* another bar with him, but—and here's the thing—he left with Alexis. He was probably talking to her all night while I was hanging out at the *Meet the Press* round-table discussion. Perhaps most disturbing of all is that Tony's my competition.

I'm quiet on the ride home. Maybe AJ's right. This is the second time Tony has asked me to an '80s concert event. It's not like I'm Rock of Ages girl just because of my dad's band. By the time AJ drops me off, I'm left feeling like I'm somewhere in between "happy crush" and "crushed" with a splash of dread at the discussion I'll be having with my parents.

"Everything okay?" AJ asks.

"Just worried about what the parents are going to say. Thanks for the ride."

"Sure," AJ says as he pulls up to my house. It seems like he wants to say more, but whatever it is or was just hangs there between us until finally he just says, "Later."

"Later."

When I walk through the door, my mom and dad are both waiting for me in the living room. This is not good, es-pecially since my mom should have been in bed hours ago.

Dad dives right in. "A bar, Sam? Really?"

"And lying?" Mom says. "You've never kept anything from us before. Is this about a boy?"

I'm mortified. "God, Mom. No. Some people were going out after work and they asked me if I wanted to go, that's all. Meg was there, Harry, AJ, all the *Herald Tribune* people."

My mom moves closer to me. "Do I smell beer? Have you been drinking?"

"All I drank was Diet Coke. Someone spilled a beer on me."

"I'm not sure I like the influence those people are having on you," Dad says.

"Maybe you should quit this job and find something with better hours," Mom says.

"I don't want to quit. I like it there."

"Well, your father and I don't like all these late nights," Mom says.

"I'm *working*. This was the only time I went to the bar."

"The bottom line is, you shouldn't have lied to your mother," Dad says.

Yeah, I see that now, my brain screams. But my lips are zipped. I'm in enough trouble.

"We'll talk more about it tomorrow," Mom says.

Yay.

"Agreed," says Dad.

I'm furious. They're the ones who wanted me to take on a challenging summer job. It was one little fib. That's what I get for being such a Goody Two-Shoes.

"Good night," Dad says, placing one hand on top of my head before he walks toward the steps.

"Love you," Mom says.

How can they both do that? Just turn the anger off and go to bed. Not me. My arms are crossed, and I refuse to make eye contact, but I mumble back, "Love you too." I'm still mad, but I would never not say that back.

What did insomniacs do before Wikipedia? My head swirls with too many thoughts, none of them good. My parents are mad and talking about making me quit the *Herald Tribune*. My crush, who may or may not be attracted to me for my knowledge of the '80s, has become my competition. And Harry makes it sound like becoming a journalist is about as practical as opening a record store.

I want to call Shelby and tell her about my night, but I can't, since I lied. Because apparently I'm a liar now. Anyway, I never heard from her again today, so I'm guessing she went to the party. Not that I care much. I'd rather that she keep busy and not get wind of the *Herald Tribune*'s bar nights.

I prop my laptop on my knees. First I check Journey's website and find out when their concert tour with Foreigner comes to New Jersey. Saturday, July 30. Then I settle in for a couple hours' worth of searching down inane facts. I type "armadilo" into the Wikipedia search engine. Of course, me being me, I misspell the critter's name and the website politely reprimands me. "Did you mean: *armadillo*?"

Of course I did, but the fact that the search engine produces the correct results even though I spelled *armadillo* with only one *l* only reinforces my belief that spelling is just not that big a deal in the twenty-first century. *In your face, Bernadette!*

I find a captivating two-minute video on YouTube of one little guy coming out of his burrow to have a look around. It's really a lot cuter than I thought. I guess I just needed to see one in action—and not petrified on Harry's shelf—to truly appreciate how oddly adorable an armadillo can be. Maybe Harry is right—they *are* misunderstood. I mean, anyone can love a bunny, but there's something I admire about an animal so peculiar looking yet so happy to be in its own skin—"skin" that resembles a coat of armor. That, in combination with his long nose, makes me think of Don Quixote tilting at windmills. I read it in my Great Books class last year.

I Google "Don Quixote," who reminds me of Harry, so then I type in "Bosnian War." (I've got Google ADD.) It's hard to believe Harry came so close to a Pulitzer and ended up at the *Herald Tribune*. Not that it's a bad newspaper. It's got a circulation of about 30,000, and under Harry the paper consistently wins awards for its news coverage. Still, it's not the *New York Times*.

For the hell of it, I Google "Sy Goldberg." It's become part of my routine. Let's see. . . . Sy Goldberg, tax consultant in Nyack, New York. Sy Goldberg of Goldberg & Goldberg Law, Sy Goldberg on various social-networking sites. None appears to be our Sy Goldberg, but then again, how would I know for sure? I'd better step up my game if I'm going to secure my spot as Michael's vacation substitute.

I put my laptop aside, pull out the spiral notebook I use as a journal, and flip to the back where I keep all the pictures and articles—duplicates of mine and others'—I cut out from magazines and newspapers.

Lately, the pages have really been piling up. I've got Anton's obit, my front-page story, and some of my favorite feature obits. I keep the picture of the dress—the perfect dress—on top. I cut it out of *Seventeen* magazine's prom issue two years ago. It's a pale yellow, strapless gown with a full, tea-length skirt. The model is wearing strands of ivory pearls around her neck, and the caption reads "Girly retro." I get lost staring at this dress. It's so sweet and light and timeless and pretty. I fantasize about walking into prom with Tony and wearing this dress. It's like nothing I've ever owned, and most people wouldn't see this dress (or any dress) and think "That's so Sam," but I love it.

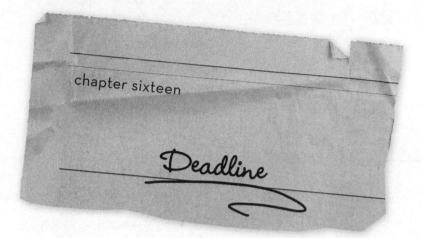

chapter sixteen

Deadline

It's the morning after bar night, and I am wiped after only four hours of sleep. I eat my Cheerios while staring through the sliding glass doors at the gnarled, asymmetrical dogwood tree in our yard. Each spring, my dad threatens to cut it down, but I always beg him not to. It's invariably the last tree to bloom. "It just needs a little more time," I tell Dad every year. While the world turns pastel around her, the dogwood stands there naked and brown like an exposed network of nerve endings, chronically out of sync. Like me.

I'm finishing breakfast and getting ready for my run when Mom walks into the kitchen, wearing yoga pants, a sea-foam–colored T-shirt and a ponytail. She's usually gone by now. I'm so surprised, I momentarily forget that I'm in for a cross-examination about last night.

"How come you're still home? Are you feeling okay?" I ask.

"Doctor's appointment," she says. Her clipped tone says, *We're not going to talk about me right now, we're going to talk about you.*

Call it the estrogen effect, but mothers and daughters can always hear the words behind the words in a seemingly normal—even dull—conversation.

"So," she says, "now you're going to bars? You told me you were working late."

"I told you I was going to be extra late. I didn't say what I was doing."

"The sneaky thing is not going to fly with me, Sam. Not if you want me to trust you."

She's right, of course. I've got to do damage control.

"I'm sorry," I say. "Please don't make me quit my job. It won't happen again."

"Your father and I talked about it." She lets out a sigh and continues. "We're happy you found a job that you truly enjoy, but *I* think you're too young to be working so much and so late."

I open my mouth to talk, but she holds up her hand. "Let me finish. So, we don't think we're asking too much when we want to know where you are and who you're with. And if you're going to be drinking—"

"Believe me, it wasn't about drinking. I told you, someone spilled beer on me. I just wanted to hang out with everyone. They go out every week."

It's mostly the truth. I wish I could tell her sneaking off to bar night had a little something to do with a boy. Shelby and her mom talk about guys all the time. Connecting with my mom that way would be nice, but I'm too embarrassed.

"I want to believe you, sweetie. But it's hard after you've already lied. That's my point."

"Okay, I get it. But if I told you I was going to a bar with people from work, would you have let me go?"

"I'm not sure, Sam. You didn't give me that chance, did you?"

"I'm sorry. I really am." I say, though I'd like to throw up my arms and yell, *It's not like I came home pregnant or have a meth addiction.* But I still don't know where I stand. "So? Are you going to make me quit?"

Mom stares hard at me before answering. "We're not going to make you quit . . . *yet.* But it better not happen again."

"It won't, Mom, I promise." I raise my hand like I'm taking the Girl Scout oath.

The tension in her face relaxes. "Okay. I believe you."

I put my cereal bowl in the dishwasher, then grab my iPod off the table. "Thank you, Mom," I say, and kiss her cheek. "I'm going to hit the treadmill before work."

"Do you want a ride? I've got some time before my doctor's appointment."

"Sure. That sounds good," I say, adjusting my earbuds. I'm about to head into the garage but change my mind. "I'm going on the street today. Be back in an hour."

Outside, I inhale the scents of freshly cut grass and the pansies lining our walk. I love how summer smells. After a quick stretch, I jog off toward the high school. I'm going to run there, do eight laps around the track, and run home. I've been planning this route for a while, I just haven't made it out of the garage. According to mapmyrun.com, it's just over six miles.

I reach Cook Street and know I've hit my first mile. Even if I hadn't plotted my course, I could tell by how many songs have played in my ears and how I feel. It's funny how my body just knows when it's ready to pick up the pace.

I run the length of Cook, cut through the new McMansion development, and turn into the high school parking lot. That's when I hear the familiar sounds of marching-band music bleeding through the alt-rock mix in my ears. Band camp. I get that queasy summer-interruptus feeling.

Lap One: The marching band is too loud. It's making me think about school. Once September comes, there are going to be exams to take, applications to fill out, colleges to visit—choices I'm not yet ready to make. I haven't gotten sixteen right yet, and now I'm going to be seventeen. I'm not ready.

Lap Two: Am I selling myself short? Should I take the SATs one more time? Apply to some tier-one colleges, like my parents have been urging?

Lap Three: Do I look for a school with highly rated journalism program? Is that what I want to do? Is that what I should do?

Lap Four: I wonder if AJ will follow the mayor with me again. Prom fantasy aside, I can't let Tony get Michael's beat, no matter how adorable he is.

Lap Five: Maybe Harry will let me keep working for the Herald Tribune *part-time once school starts.*

———

Back at home, I'm proud of myself for completing my first 10k *outside*. But my runner's high is tempered by thoughts of my job ending and my senior year beginning. I need a game plan, for both.

"Morning, Gram," I say, reaching into the fridge for some water. She's at the kitchen table doing her crossword puzzle, her daily ritual.

"Morning, hon," my grandmother says as she gets up and heads toward the Mr. Coffee to refill her mug. "What's wrong? You look so serious."

"It's just my face, Gram," I say. "Permanently morose."

"Morose? You? You're just not a morning person. We can't all greet the day with alacrity," Gram says. "Your great-aunt Mary, God rest her soul, now, she was morose. She was the real crepe hanger of the family. She could turn Christmas into a funeral."

"Crepe hanger?" I'll look up *alacrity* later.

"Back when I was a girl, when a family member died, you hung a black funeral drape over the door," Gram explains. "It let other people know that someone had died."

I need to write down some of these tidbits before I forget and Gram's not here to ask anymore. There I go. Being morose again.

"Sometimes I just want to be a normal teenager," I say. It's a non sequitur to her crepe-hanger anecdote, but I need to say it aloud. I should have wanted to be at Rob McGinty's party last night, wearing a strapless top and doing beer funnels. But honestly, I was where I wanted to be.

"I raised four kids, and I can tell you one thing, hon: Teenagers are not normal." And then Gram comes over and gives me a big, squishy hug. I resist at first.

"Ah, Gram. I'm all sweaty."

"Oh, come on, that doesn't bother me." I put my arms around her and hug her back, happy she can give me just what I need and we don't have to talk about it.

———

An hour later, Mom pulls up in front of the the *Herald Tribune* building. "Thanks, Mom."

"Be careful," my mom says as I open the door. "I'd say come home early, but I have a feeling I'd be wasting my breath."

"Okay, I'll try. Thanks for the ride, Mom," I say. "Why are you going to the doctor's today, anyway?"

"Just a routine physical," she says.

I should have asked sooner. Is Mom worried something may be wrong with her?

"Well, good luck. I'll call you later," I say.

"Love you," she says.

"Love you too," I say.

———

A J is already at his desk when I arrive. I glance at the clock. Am I late? Nope. Right on time.

"It's Thursday," I blurt.

"It is." AJ is nonplussed by my randomness.

"We followed the mayor to the bank on a Wednesday."

"I'm going to have to trust you on that one."

"It was. I know because it was the day I made my big obit gaff."

"Right. Okay, then. Glad we cleared that up."

AJ goes back to typing.

"So, I'm thinking—"

He pauses then, takes his glasses off, and cleans them on his shirttail. "Here we go."

"People usually do their banking on the same day every week. Gram does hers on Friday, when the Social Security check arrives, and—"

"I'm begging you, Sam-I-am, get to the point."

"Maybe we should start following the mayor on Wednesday afternoons."

"Fine."

"Really? That was easy. I thought it would take more convincing."

"I said 'fine,' didn't I? Don't make me take it back."

"Great! Thanks! So next Wednesday—"

"Sam . . ."

"Right. Got it."

I skitter off to Alice's desk and pick up the mail, happy to have a plan in motion.

———

After lunch, Harry stands on Rocco's desk to make an announcement. "Listen up, people. Mandatory meeting in the conference room at three," he yells. "Spread the word to anyone who's not here."

"Any idea what that's about?" I ask AJ.

"No clue."

Curiosity may kill cats, but journalists aren't far behind. Grace wonders if Harry is resigning, Jack thinks his features staff is being cut, Jim from sports guesses it's about another pay freeze.

At three, we all cram into the conference room like clowns in a compact car, ready to find out. Every seat is taken. The sports guys are sitting on the bookshelves, which run the length of the room along the windows. AJ is next to them, and he waves me over and points to the spot he saved for me. Everyone else, including our three burly press guys—Dan, Henry, and Franco—is standing. Harry, with hair looking crazier than usual, is at his seat at the head of the conference table. The phone is in front of him.

"Alice, let's dial up Bernie. She should hear this," he says. After a minute or so, Alice turns the phone toward Harry.

"I'm putting you on speaker now, Bernie. Hold on," Alice says.

"Harry!" booms Bernie. She sounds like she's locked in the bathroom. Oh, how I've missed that voice.

"Bernie, I hear you'll be rejoining us soon. Looking forward to it."

"Oh, man," I whisper. It's great that Bernie is recovering and all, but her return means we're back to being Moron and Moronica. I catch AJ's eye. I can tell he's thinking the same thing.

"All right, listen up. The publisher and I have been enjoying many breakfast meetings together this summer at the Tick Tock Diner. After extensive negotiations with several potential buyers, he has decided to sell our small group of newspapers to a larger media conglomerate."

"What does that mean for us?" Michael asks.

"I'm getting there, Fishman. I'm getting there."

Harry takes a deep breath. He looks tired. More tired than I've ever seen him look.

"For starters, it means layoffs. We're cutting our workforce by forty percent. There are three papers in our group. A total of a hundred and twenty-five editorial jobs. You will all have the opportunity to apply for the seventy-five remaining positions." The news sends a wave of grumbling throughout the conference room. Selfishly, I wonder if this dashes any hopes I had about continuing to work here during the school year. It's like the escape hatch from high school is closing.

"Okay, settle down," Harry says. "There's more. This is important."

"We're shifting our format to more online content and substantially reducing the size of the print version. I'd like all of you to start thinking about content that will drive people to our site. Blogs, message boards, columns, smartphone apps. We're changing our entire business model, and while it's probably a good thing to bring the *Herald Tribune* into the twenty-first century, this last change will be the most difficult of all: We will be shutting down our presses at the end of August and sending the paper out for printing. I am not exaggerating when I tell you it will be the end of an era."

With that, all eyes fall on the press guys—Dan, Henry, and Franco. They're all pushing sixty and have been doing this job most of their lives. It's not like their skill set has prepared them for a career switch at this stage of the game.

"I want all of you here at five in the morning on the day we shut the presses down. Mandatory. That's all for now. See me about any individual questions or concerns." People start exiting the conference room, but Harry calls us back. "I almost forgot." He walks over to the wall, where I notice someone (Harry, I'm sure) has mounted a rectangular countdown clock, like the kind in Times Square on

New Year's Eve. He hits the switch, and it starts counting backward from 1334 hours 00 minutes 00 seconds until the last day of August. I think about all I want to accomplish by summer's end. It's like me and the printing presses are on the same deadline schedule.

chapter seventeen

Movie Times

On Friday night, Shelby arrives at my house at seven o'clock with the chocolate Twizzlers, peanut M&Ms, and Diet Cherry Coke—all required, she insists, for a night of movie watching. I left work promptly at five thirty today. I'm trying to earn back my parents' trust. Mom swung by the *Herald Tribune* and picked me up on her way home from work.

I make popcorn, and then the four of us—me, Shelby, Mom, and Gram—settle in the family room to watch a movie. Mom and I are on one couch, Gram and Shelby share the other. Our snacks are spread before us on ottomans that double as tables by flipping the cushions over.

"You girls ready for the eighties experience?" Mom says.

"Let's start with *The Breakfast Club*, then *Sixteen Candles*," I say.

"Two movies? Is Shelby going to sit still that long?" Gram jokes.

Shelby throws up her arms. "Thank you!"

"Okay, fine," I say. "Just *Sixteen Candles* then."

I should be happy to have a friend who doesn't mind staying in on a Friday night to watch movies with me, my mom, and my grandmother, but the truth is, movie marathons are my thing with Mom. Shelby called me at work to see if I wanted to go out, and I felt bad blowing her off again.

Mom puts the DVD in the player. "You're going to like this," she says. "All my friends were in love with Jake Ryan."

I grab a handful of popcorn and slip into my comfort zone. I don't think about yesterday's announcement at the *Herald Tribune*, the search for Sy Goldberg, my driving test looming in August, and school starting after Labor Day. I get lost in this hilarious romantic story about a girl named Samantha, who has a major crush on a gorgeous, popular senior named Jake. Relate much? The last scene is killer. Jake spends half the movie looking for Sam because it turns out he likes her too. She comes out of the church, where her sister has just gotten married, and is standing on the steps in her poufy bridesmaid dress watching the guests leave. When the last car pulls away, it's like the big reveal! There is Jake, leaning against a red Porsche, waiting for her. I am melting. John Hughes *was* a genius.

"Why can't that happen to us?" Shelby says as she

chews the tip of her straw, like she's done since we were kids.

"As much as I love your dad, nothing that romantic has ever happened to me," Mom says. She's already off the couch and loading the dishwasher.

"Real love doesn't drive up in a red sports car," Gram says. "When you finally find the right one, it's so simple. You won't believe you never saw it before."

"Was it love at first sight with Gramps?" I ask.

"Yeah, did you know right away you wanted to marry him?" Shelby asks.

"Right away?" She laughs. "It took ten years. Longer, if you count the time when we were just kids. I grew up with your grandfather. We were neighbors, so I really didn't think of him that way."

"When did things change?" Mom asks.

"I suppose when I was old enough to start dating. There were so many times when I'd come home after a night out, and there he was, sitting on my porch."

"Really? What was he doing there?" I ask.

"That's what I always wanted to know." Gram chuckles at the memory. "He always said the same thing: 'Waiting for you.' Oh, sometimes he'd be inside playing cards with my brothers, but most of the time, he was on the front porch."

"That might be considered stalking by today's standards," Shelby says.

"You could be right," Gram says.

"So, what made you finally want to go out with him?" Mom asks.

"Well, I was engaged to another man at the time. Joe. He gave me a ring and everything. I hid it on my bookshelf. I told no one except your grandfather. He was my best friend, I suppose," she says. "I even showed him the ring."

"You were *engaged*? So, what happened?" I am riveted. My grandmother almost married another man? She *dated*? Who knew? Mom looks as shocked as I am.

"It was Easter Sunday. I'd bought a new dress, gloves, and matching shoes. Oh, and a beautiful hat—we all wore hats back then," she says. "Joe was supposed to take me to church and then have dinner with my family."

"What happened?" Mom asks.

"Joe said he was going to New York with his friends instead and wouldn't be able to see me until later that evening." She waves her hand, as if to swat Joe away. "I told him, 'Joe, you *go* with your friends, and don't bother coming around,' and then I walked next door and knocked on your grandfather's door."

"Gramps caught a break that day?"

"Yes, he did," Gram says. "When I told your grandfather Joe went out with his friends, he said, 'I'm glad he did.' We got married a year later."

My grandparents were together three times longer than I have been alive. I wonder if anyone will ever love me the way my grandfather loved my grandmother. The way they loved each other.

No disrespect to John Hughes, but Gram's story was better than the movie.

———

On Saturday, I return to the bookstore solo, laptop in hand. Yes, I'm on a sort of stakeout, but I heard what Harry said about coming up with online-content ideas, and I want to do some brainstorming. Perhaps he'd let me do a blog for teens, and then I could keep working at the *Herald Tribune.* I need an amazing idea to pitch to Harry.

I sit facing the door at a table toward the back, power up my laptop, and get started. I do a search of existing blogs using key words like *teens, girls, high school, punk fashion, college music, YA book reviews*—whatever pops into my head. I wind up reading tons of posts, everything from tips on writing college-application essays to toxic shock syndrome. I come to the conclusion that I can blog about almost anything, but it's better if I focus. What should the point of my blog be? Do I have enough to say? Two hours later, I look up to see Joanne and company settling into a table near mine.

"Hey," I say.

"Hi, Sam," Joanne says. "Missy, Sarah, and I have made this our new favorite place. Fiona should be starting her shift soon."

"That's cool. It's a good place to come to get ideas."

"Are you doing something for work?" Sarah asks. "Fiona mentioned you're writing for the *Herald Tribune.*"

"I guess. Sort of." I hesitate, wondering if I want to share what I'm doing with this bunch. "I'm trying to come up with an idea for a blog. For kids our age."

This gets Missy going. "I follow this blog by a girl who dishes about all the kids in her high school. She doesn't use real names or anything."

"How do you know she's not lying? She might not even be in high school," I say.

"She could be a *he*," Joanne offers.

"Burst my bubble, why don't you." Missy laughs. "I don't care. It's still entertaining."

"What do you want to write about?" Sarah asks.

"I'm still trying to decide. I want it to help readers, and I want it to be the truth," I say.

I spend the next hour tossing around ideas with Joanne, Sarah, and Missy. They're a big help, and I find I really enjoy talking with them. Shelby's topics of conversation are limited to boys, clothes, parties, and . . . well, that about covers it.

By the time I leave the coffee shop, the thought of writing for the yearbook and *Folio* this year is sounding a lot better.

chapter eighteen

News Brief

The next couple of weeks fly by in a repetitive cycle of work punctuated by running, mayor stakeouts, parent-approved bar nights, and coffee-shop visits. The latter is not so much about stalking the mayor. More and more, I'm finding I enjoy hanging out there on a regular basis with the yearbook crowd and working on ideas for my yet-to-be-launched blog. It's beginning to look like I can actually make it happen. I haven't asked the still-jobless Shelby to join me on my trips to Bargain Books & Beans. I feel a bit guilty, like I'm cheating or something, but I don't see Shelby and those girls mixing.

Shelby and I do get to the beach once. She's baffled by how I don't want to have more summer fun. But what she doesn't get is, I *am* having fun. A romance is heating up between her and the keg boy, Mark, though, so lately she's not as bothered by my lack of availability.

I've been more determined than ever to impress Harry with my feature obits. I want to prove to him I can do exceptional work on the obit desk before I approach him with my blog idea. And the cool thing is, I'm hitting my stride. It's amazing, the things people share with me, a stranger. The memories my questions trigger; the simplest details that make them laugh or cry. I've learned the importance of listening patiently. I let people talk, and wait for that one quote that sparks an idea for a lead and gives me something to build a story around.

My father always used to say he wanted us kids to have roots and wings. . . .

Every Sunday, she sat and peeled ten pounds of potatoes, ten pounds. . . .

I can't imagine not hearing him play piano anymore. . . .

My goal is to write a story people will clip from the newspaper and keep with their other mementos, something they will read ten years from now and smile at, or laminate like that woman Eileen Abraham. Yes, only the rich and famous get feature obits in newspapers like the *New York Times,* but at the *Herald Tribune,* everyone has a shot at getting his or her story told by me. It feels awesome.

The amount of fan mail I get from appreciative relatives is surprising. It's not varsity softball or the lead in a school play, but I'll take it. At the last bar night, some reporters—and even a couple of old-guy Harp regulars, like Bob and Sharkey—told me they really look forward to my feature obits. And much to my utter shock and surprise, Bernadette called last week to pay me a compliment in her own way.

"Moronica," she said when I picked up the phone, "keep it up. You finally figured out you're writing about a life, not reporting a death."

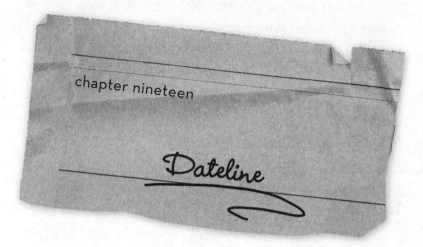

chapter nineteen

Dateline

It's the last Wednesday in July, and I've earned my shot at covering Michael's beat while he's on vacation. Harry made it official yesterday, when Michael left for Maine. Even though the news caused Tony to leave early in a huff—no pit stop by my desk to congratulate me—I smile every time I think about it.

"Are we still on after work?" AJ says, referring to our weekly "date" following the mayor.

I smile every time I think of that, too. We've determined that Wednesday is not always the mayor's banking day. Last week we wound up following him to his house, but we've gotten better about timing a food pickup with our stealth operation.

"Yep, we're on. I plan on finishing the feature obit early."

"Nice. These have been the best weeks of my life at the *Herald Tribune*," AJ says.

AJ has been able to write more music-related articles since I've been taking care of all the feature obits. His features are very well written, and Harry has stopped by the obit desk on several occasions to tell AJ he's impressed. One time, Harry actually used the word "talented." Probably why AJ's been such a good sport about helping me with this mayor business.

"Your review of that local band was excellent," I say. "I love the way you describe music. Not like those reviewers who care more about making obscure musical references than doing justice to the band. You could totally have a career as a music writer if the whole drummer thing doesn't pan out."

"Yeah?" He tries not to smile. "Thanks. Harry liked it too."

At three o'clock, I'm surprised when Alice calls my phone to say there's someone here who wants to see me. When I step into the reception area, Antoinette at the front desk nods her head toward an old—make that very, very old—man seated in one of our mustard-colored leather chairs that's almost as old as he is. He's wearing long sleeves, even though it feels like it's a hundred degrees out today with this humidity.

He stands when he sees me. "Samantha?"

"Yes."

"You are so young!" he exclaims. I'm not offended. To him, everyone must look young.

"Can I help you, sir?"

I see he's holding some papers in his hand. On top is a feature obituary I wrote last week.

"I like your writing," he says, pointing to my byline.

"Thank you."

"I am Aleksandr Kovalevsky. Alex," he says, extending his age-spot-covered hand, which I promptly take. "I would like for you to tell my story."

Then he slips another paper from the stack he's carrying. It's a faded photocopy of a newspaper clipping depicting a hollow-cheeked young man in a dirty prison uniform.

"This is me," he says. "On the day I was liberated from a Nazi prison camp. I've never told anyone about what happened to me. But now I want my grandchildren to know this story. Before I'm gone."

It takes me a few beats to process this, and I'm not sure how to proceed. Thankfully, Antoinette, who's all ears at this point, offers me a next step.

"Why don't you take this gentleman to the conference room and get him some water," she says.

I do as she suggests, then find Harry to let him know about Mr. Kovalevsky. He looks around the newsroom, and I'm wondering if he's trying to choose a reporter to go talk to him. "Meg!" he finally says. "Do you have a recorder D'Angelo can borrow?"

"Sure!"

"Grab a notebook and pen, D'Angelo. Take notes and record him too," Harry says.

"You want *me* to interview him?"

"Of course. I want to know what he has to say. Don't you?"

I do.

Meg gives me a quick lesson in how to operate her digital recorder, and I return to Mr. Kovalevsky in the conference room.

"Do you mind if I record you?" I ask.

"Not at all, my dear." The term of endearment sounds sweet coming from him and instantly puts me at ease. I flip open my notebook, pull up a chair, and turn on the recorder. I just start with the obvious question.

"How did you end up in a Nazi prison camp?"

He looks out the window. His pale blue eyes match the summer sky. Is he having second thoughts about telling me his story? But then he rubs his hands together like he's warming them and begins to speak.

"It's funny. I started off at a Russian work camp. The Germans were the ones who *liberated* me," he says. "I had no idea how much worse my nightmare would become."

His story unfolds like a Spielberg film. The son of Ukrainian immigrants, Kovalevsky went to visit his grandmother in Poland in 1939. He was there during the Soviet invasion and eventually imprisoned when KGB officers stormed his grandmother's home and found his American flag in her house. "My prison cell was very, very dark. Many mornings I would awake and think I had gone blind," he says. He takes a drink of water, and I wait for him to speak again. I ask very few questions—he's had a long time to think about this story. All I do is listen. "One of my favorite things to think about was the parade I attended after Charles Lindbergh made his transatlantic flight. I relived that day many, many times."

His days were divided, he says, between walking in circles in his solitary cell and interrogations, where he was forced to stand at attention for hours with a bright light shining in his face. And throughout it all, he was literally starving, given only "filthy soup" to eat.

In 1941, Mr. Kovalevsky was liberated when the Germans invaded eastern Poland, but eventually sent to a Nazi camp, where he remained until the end of the war. I can't believe what he endured for all those years. He was beaten, starved, humiliated, and again interrogated. He saw mass graves and witnessed men being nailed to concrete walls and pregnant women being tortured and left for dead. These memories, he says, still wake him up screaming in the middle of the night.

"I'm getting up in age. I didn't want my story to die with me," he says. "It wasn't easy to find people who wanted to listen to me when the war ended. A lot of people had sad stories. But I want my family to know what happened to me."

After his liberation, he married and had three children. He has six grandchildren and a great-grandchild on the way. But no one knows the details of his imprisonment. How many stories get lost because people didn't want to listen or ask questions? Mr. Kovalevsky's makes me think about the history that dies when an elderly person passes away. My own grandmother was a young girl when World War II ended, and she and her family had survived the Great Depression, but most of the time, all I ever ask her about is what's on TV or what we're having for dinner.

Nearly two hours later, I walk Mr. Kovalevsky to the reception area. "Thank you, Samantha," he says, grabbing my hand with both of his. His eyes are watery, and I'm afraid if he starts crying, I will too.

"Thank you," I say. "I'm honored you chose me to talk to."

As I watch him walk gingerly through the glass doors and down the sidewalk, I'm sad and drained but also inspired. I can't change the horrible things that happened to him, but I can tell other people what this man endured in order to live.

As I pass by Harry on the way to my desk, he looks up and says, "How'd it go?"

"Intense. He had a lot to say."

"Take your time with it," Harry says. "Get me something by next Friday and we'll go from there."

That gives me more than a week. I'm glad. A lot of my best writing happens in my head. Stories form and organize themselves there. The quotes I remember are usually the ones worth keeping. I've come to realize that journalists, the really good ones, aren't just great wordsmiths, they're great thinkers.

"Where've ya been?" AJ asks when I sit down at my

desk. I fill him in and get the usual one-word AJ response of "heavy." He packs a lot of emotion into two syllables.

"I don't have to file the story tonight, though," I say.

"Okay. Let me finish this concert preview and we can go."

I start transcribing my notes while AJ finishes working, and that's when Tony stops by my desk.

"Hey, Sam," he says. "I forgot to tell you. I'm leaving earlier than expected for my vacation, so I won't be going to the Journey and Foreigner concert on Saturday."

I've been so busy, I'd forgotten all about it. Almost.

"Oh, that's okay. Thanks for letting me know."

"Alexis is still going. Maybe you can be her plus one."

Still going? So, she was invited all along? I shrug it off.

"Uh, no. That's all right. Have fun in Aruba."

My body feels hot. I can't look at AJ after Tony walks away.

"Thanks, I will." Tony smiles like a cat with a canary in his mouth.

"You were going to be Coma Boy's plus one?!"

Oh, here we go. "No! He mentioned it a long time ago. I completely forgot about it. And, anyway, I don't remember ever saying I'd go."

"No explanation necessary," AJ says. "Date whomever you want."

My back goes up when he says that. I *can* date anyone I want. It's not like AJ shares any information about his love life with me. I never did find out what he was doing with

Jessica in Chestnutville during the weekend of the Fourth. We spend enough time together at work and on weekly stakeouts—if at any point he wanted to hang out as more than just friends, well, he's a big boy. He should have said something.

I don't talk much as we follow the mayor's Jaguar to his final destination, Fidelity Savings in Belleville—we got lucky, today is banking day. The quiet time gives me a chance to think. When AJ parks the car, I decide to shake things up a bit. I wait until the mayor leaves through the back door, the one closest to the parking lot, and I get out of the car.

"Come on," I say to AJ. "Let's go in the front."

When we get through the doors, I run up to a teller and act like I'm out of breath.

"Hi! We were supposed to meet our new boss here. I don't have an account yet, but he said he would cash our paychecks for us. We work at his bookstore slash coffee shop."

"Was he here? Big guy? Salt-and-pepper hair?" AJ asks.

"You mean Mr. Goldberg?" the teller says. "He just walked out the back door. Maybe you can catch him in the parking lot."

"Thank you!" I say, then I grab AJ by the arm. "Come on."

By the time we get to the lot, the mayor is long gone. Still, I wait until we're back in the car before I say anything.

"Why is the mayor pretending to be Sy Goldberg? Is Sy too sick to sign paychecks?" I ask.

"Maybe he's stealing Sy's money while the poor guy lies dying."

"I know I should tell Harry, but I can't. He told me to stay out of it, and I don't want him to get mad at me before my big week of covering Michael's beat."

"Wait until Michael gets back. We're not sure what this means or what it proves. If anything," AJ says.

"I guess." The guilt may give me an ulcer by then.

"It can wait a week," AJ says. "Trust me."

I do trust AJ.

———

It's Friday morning, and I'm flying solo at East Passaic city hall this morning. My dad dropped me off here at ten, and AJ agreed to pick me up when I'm done. I've already stopped by the police and fire department headquarters and the mayor's office. Just like Meg showed me. Mayor Amato wasn't in this time, but I got my advance copy of the agenda of the next city council meeting from his secretary, Marisol.

I'm about to text AJ to say I'll meet him out front in five minutes when I realize I forgot to charge my phone. I glance around the maze of cubicles and spy an empty one. The nameplate reads KIKI RAMIREZ. Sounds like she should be famous, not stuck behind a desk in city hall. I walk over to the man across from Kiki's.

"Excuse me," I say. "Would it be okay if I use the phone on Kiki Ramirez's desk? It's a local call, and it doesn't look like—"

"Who?" He looks confused. I may have woken him up.

"Kiki? She sits across from you?"

"I've never seen anybody sitting there," the man says. He's standing now and looking toward the cubicle in question. "As far as I know, no one sits there."

"Oh, well, could I use the phone? I'll be quick."

"Okay by me. Dial nine for an outside line." Then he sits down and goes back to work or his nap. I'm not sure which.

Fifteen minutes later, it feels like I'm stepping into a sauna when I walk through the front doors of city hall and into the heavy August air. AJ is already waiting by the curb. It's a shame the air-conditioning doesn't work in his Jeep. I'm going to be a sweaty mess by the time I get to the *Herald Tribune*.

I open the passenger door and get inside.

"Hey," I say.

"Hey."

"Got the agenda." I wave the document in his face, then buckle my seat belt.

"Anything look interesting?"

"I don't think so. I'll have Meg double-check it for me. Tuesday's meeting should be a short one. Feel like coming with me? We can hit the Harp afterward," I say.

"You mean you want me to be your plus one?"

I slap him with the agenda.

Is this a dig about Tony, or does he want it to be a date? Do I? It now feels like it's about 107 degrees in his vehicle, because I'm blushing. But I don't think AJ notices. For the rest of the ride, he never looks my way.

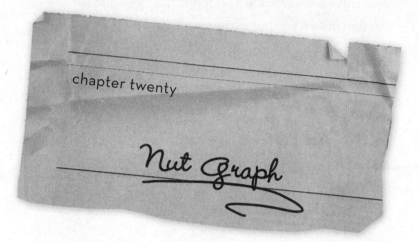

chapter twenty

Nut Graph

I spent all day yesterday prepping for this Tuesday-night city-council meeting. Meg read over the agenda again with me to see if there are any important votes coming up. The only thing that seems newsworthy is a cost-savings proposal to go from two-day-a-week garbage pickup to one. Perhaps the city's tax dollars would be better spent if it focused its trash-removal efforts on the mayor.

Before I leave for the meeting, Meg shows me how to prewrite the trash story, including nut graphs—paragraphs that give some history and bring readers up to speed about why the story is news. When AJ and I walk into the council chambers, I've got my laptop, my notebook, and Meg's recorder. I'm ready.

The council shares space with the municipal court. Reporters sit at the table used for the defense. The seven-member council sits behind an elongated judge's bench, and there's a lectern at the top of the aisle for the public portion of the meeting when citizens are allowed to address the council. So far, the only spectators here are me, AJ, a reporter from the *Record-Gazette* (our competition), and an older gentleman in a robin's-egg blue seersucker suit who came in carrying a briefcase.

"That's Constantine," the *Record-Gazette* reporter whispers to me. "Never misses a meeting. Thinks he's an attorney."

Ah. Michael warned me about him. His exact words were, *Do not make eye contact with Constantine. He's like a half-wit cobra. He won't stop talking and you'll miss your deadline.* Apparently, Constantine shows up at city hall every day too. Michael says he's gotten some good tips on stories from him, but often, since he's a few cards short of a deck, it's not always easy to figure out what Constantine really knows and what he's making up.

The meeting drags on and on. The council votes on various resolutions related to the mundane business of running a city; Constantine makes an impressive presentation on trash collection, complete with visuals; AJ sneaks off to the back row to pop in his earbuds and falls asleep. And then, just when it seems like the meeting is wrapping up, the city attorney blindsides me.

"The mayor would like to make a motion to discuss a personnel matter behind closed doors."

"Can they do that?" I ask the *Record-Gazette* reporter.

"Yep. For personnel matters, they're allowed to close

the meeting." He starts packing up his stuff. "This could take the rest of the night. I'm out of here."

I quick dial the city desk and get Grace. I tell her what's going on and ask her what I should do.

"Ask them what the personnel matter is related to," she says. "You're entitled to that information."

I hang up just as they're about to take a vote to go into closed session. The *Record-Gazette* reporter is already gone. AJ is in la-la land. I panic. I raise my hand like I'm in school, stand up, and start talking. "Uh, hello. I'm Samantha D'Angelo from the *Herald Tribune*." Did the mayor smirk when I mentioned the paper's name? *Jerk.* "Can I ask what the personnel matter relates to? This wasn't on the agenda I picked up."

"It's in reference to filling an anticipated vacancy on the weatherization board."

"Sy Goldberg's position?" I blurt out. The mayor definitely scowls when he hears me mention the name.

"We're not at liberty to discuss that information," the city attorney says. "And now, if the council is ready to vote, will someone make a motion to move into private session?"

I'm already dialing Grace back to tell her what's going on. "Wait there until it's over," she says. "If they take any kind of vote, it still has to be in public."

"Got it." I look at the time. Ten o'clock. My parents aren't going to like this. But when I call my mom to tell her I'm going to be late, even though she's not thrilled, she's happy AJ is with me. I look over at him. Eyes closed, arms folded across his chest. His T-shirt is riding up in the front, exposing his navel and tight lower abs. All of a sudden I get warm and tingly watching him sleep. Too bad I've got to wake him. I slide along the back row and nudge his knee with mine. He opens one eye.

"Is it over? Sweet."

"No. They're meeting in closed chambers on a personnel matter. I have a feeling it has something to do with Sy Goldberg. Grace wants me to stay. You've got to find that Constantine guy before he leaves and talk to him—"

"Whoa, whoa, and whoa." He runs his fingers through his long hair. "Who is Constantine?"

"The kooky guy in the blue suit. I need you to ask him if he's heard anything about who the mayor is trying to hire to replace Sy Goldberg with. Maybe he thinks Michael will back off if Sy resigns for health reasons. I bet he planned this whole thing for when Michael wouldn't be here."

AJ puts a hand on my shoulder. "Relax. You need to find something besides Sy Goldberg to get all hot and bothered about."

"Can you go see if Constantine is hanging around in the hall? I'll stay here in case the council comes out to vote on anything. Please, AJ."

"Fine. I'm goin'."

Twenty minutes later, AJ returns to find me. I've had to endure three texts from Shelby. The first two both said the same thing:

Hello where R U?

The third said,

Is this thing on?

Must be a slow party night in Chestnutville.

"You so owe me," AJ says. "People trippin' on acid make more sense than that old dude."

"Did you find out anything?"

He smiles. "What's it worth to you?

"AJ!"

"Okay, okay. You were right. This *is* about your boyfriend, Sy Goldberg. Seems like he's resigning from the board if he doesn't kick first. The mayor wants to replace him with some chick named Kiki Ramirez."

"Holy crap! I know that name."

"You're delirious."

"I'm serious." I tell him about the empty cubicle in city hall with Kiki Ramirez's nameplate on it. "The guy who sits across from her said as far as he knew, it's always been empty."

"Convenient. The mayor's replacing one no-show employee with another," AJ says.

"Bingo!"

I flip open my laptop. First I Google "Kiki Ramirez." Too many hits. *Kiki Ramirez on Twitter, Kiki Ramirez on LinkedIn, on YouTube* . . . What did I expect to find? I'm about to refine my search when I spot a Kiki Ramirez on some site called Eternal Obits, a place where one can honor one's ancestors. That triggers something in my brain. How far back do the *Herald Tribune*'s online obits go?

"What are you doing? Let's go." AJ whines.

"Just a sec," I say. "Grace said we have to stay put a while longer anyway."

I pull up the archives search on the *Herald Tribune*'s website. I search for Kiki Ramirez.

"You're not going to believe this!" I say.

I turn my screen toward AJ. He reads: " 'Kiki Ramirez, age twelve, died Thursday.' Wow. She was young. A kid."

"What's the date on the obit?" I ask.

"January tenth, 2005," AJ says. "Do you think it's the same person? Is the mayor replacing a dying person with a dead person?"

"Not exactly. Maybe Sy and Kiki have more in common than a job," I say.

"Whataya mean?"

"I mean, I don't think Sy Goldberg is dying. I think he's already dead."

"Identity theft. So, it's not the mayor's cronies collecting salaries for no-show jobs, it's him."

"That's what I'm thinking. Gram told me about this. She saw it on *Dateline*. It's scary how easy it is to steal the identities of dead people."

"It's scary how many hours a day you spend thinking about this stuff."

I ignore AJ and begin typing names into the *Herald Tribune*'s search engine. I type in "Sy Goldberg," "Sydney Golberg," "Sylvan Golberg." Nothing. I try to recall the other names I found on those baby-name websites . . . Synclair, Sythe, Syahid. Still nothing.

"I don't get it. Why don't we have an obit for Sy?"

"Just because Sy Goldberg isn't in our database doesn't mean he's not dead," AJ says. "It depends on where and when he died. Our archives don't go back very far. Here, let me see your computer."

AJ does a search for "Social Security numbers for the deceased" and comes up with something called the Social Security Death Index.

"Who knew something like this even existed?" I say.

"He'd need Social Security numbers to put them on the payroll."

I take the laptop back from AJ.

First I plug in my grandfather's name, Vincenzo D'Angelo, just to see how it works. There are 2,160 results, but I can narrow the results by county, state, and date of death, all of which I know. I plug in the information and get an exact match.

I search Sy Goldberg. Again, I get a ton of results. But then, just for kicks, I type in Passaic County, New Jersey, and click the button that says "match all terms exactly."

"Look at this!" I scream at AJ. "There's an exact match for a Sy Goldberg who died in Passaic County, New Jersey, in 1964. It has his year of birth too, 1947."

"So, he would have been only seventeen. With all the dead people in the world, why would he be stupid enough to steal the identities of local dead people?" AJ wonders aloud.

"Maybe he had good reason to believe he wouldn't get caught. So far, he's been right."

Next I plug in Kiki Ramirez. There are more than 39,000 results. AJ leans over my shoulder and looks at the screen. His proximity makes my heart pound against my ribs, and for some reason, I'm holding my breath.

"Should I refine the search with the details from the obit I found in the *Herald Tribune*'s archives?" I ask.

"You could, but that's not going to help. What we really need is to match the Social Security numbers the city has on record for Sy and Kiki with a match in the Death Registry."

"Yeah, and don't forget the bank account for Sy," I say. "The mayor would have needed a Social Security number for that, too."

It's almost eleven thirty when we wrap up our online research for the night. The council never came out again to take a vote. I didn't think they would. Before I send Grace the trash-removal story, I give her a rapid-fire version of what AJ and I suspect the mayor is doing.

"Maybe we should call Harry tonight?"

"I'll reach out to him," Grace says. "You two go on home, but be prepared to meet with Harry first thing in the morning."

"Got it." I hang up with Grace and turn to AJ. I'm so excited, I don't think I'll be able to sleep. "Did you still want to stop by the Harp? I know I promised when I asked you—"

"Isn't it kind of late?"

"Uh, yeah, I guess, but I don't think my parents will mind. Unless you don't want to—I totally understand. . . ." I'm flustered as I gather up my stuff. Loose strands of hair that have escaped from my ponytail fall across my face. My hands are full, so I twist my mouth and try to blow the wisps out of my eye.

AJ reaches over and tucks the hair behind my ear. His fingers linger there for a split second. My mouth goes dry.

"Come on, Sam-I-am," hc says. "Let's get you home."

———————

Harry, AJ, and I are sitting in the conference room. We've told Harry everything. About last night's meeting; following the mayor on banking days; Shelby's application at the coffee shop; and, most important, about how we believe Mayor Amato is stealing identities of dead people and putting them on the city payroll. Now we've got Michael on speakerphone, calling us from his vacation in Bar Harbor. I feel bad that Harry bothered him, but I knew he'd want to hear this. He's soon brought up to speed.

"So, the Wonder Twins over here think they've uncovered an identity-theft scheme. The mayor's got bigger cojones than I thought," Harry says. "Why don't you run the names of any other city employees you suspect of having no-show jobs through the death registry? See what you find."

"Will do," Michael says.

A link between the mayor, the money, and the Social Security numbers of the dead people has to be established. For that we need the city to give us its employee payroll records, which Harry thinks will ultimately require law-enforcement subpoena power. Harry says he will eventually be turning over what we discovered to the U.S. Attorney's Office for the District of New Jersey, but not until Michael does enough digging to get us a kick-ass page-one story on the mayor and his invisible employees.

"Unbelievable. I can't believe I'm ten hours away and missing all this," Michael says.

"Enjoy what's left of your vacation, Fishman. Your ass is mine when you get back. I want the story."

Then he turns toward us, or maybe *on* us.

"And you two. If intern scum duties aren't keeping you busy enough, I've got something that will. You're both going to do a complete inventory of the library. We need to know what we've got back there. After we shut the presses down, this building may be next to go."

"Great," AJ mumbles.

"What's that, Sherlock Holmes?" Harry asks.

"Coffee?" I offer.

"That's what I thought," Harry says. "A lightly buttered bagel would be nice too."

After we get back from the deli, I spend what's left of the morning amid stacks of yellowed newspapers, reference books made obsolete by the Internet, small filing cabinets containing microfilmed copies of the *Herald Tribune*, and six large filing cabinets jammed with old photos used in the days before digital photography. The library.

Harry wants the photos organized first, which would be no problem if I were a CIA agent with a background in code cracking. But I'm not. For example, under *S* one would expect to find, oh, I don't know, *Saturday Night Live*, Sex Pistols, sunsets—anything at all beginning with the letter *S*. Instead I find pictures of President John F. Kennedy, his brother Bobby, John Lennon, Martin Luther King Jr., and Dimebag Darrell from the heavy-metal band Pantera. Why?! The answer is found scrawled in red Sharpie on the back of each photo. All are labeled SHOT DEAD. Really!? The whole process is taking *forever*. My nose and throat already feel permanently coated with dust. Worse yet, AJ and I will be working in shifts, since one of us needs to stay near the phones, so I'm stuck doing library cleanup alone.

Before lunch, I take a break from the photos and tackle the yearbooks. My plan is to group them by high school and then put them in date order. Right now, they seem to be organized by color—color me surprised.

As I'm stacking the Northside High School yearbooks, my eyes fall on the one with pictures of Anton, the boy who died in the fire. I can't help myself. I flip to the page with the track team and smiling Anton. It's so hard to believe the boy in this photo is gone. School will be starting in a few weeks without him, I wonder how his friends feel. Maybe I can write about Anton in my blog.

After Paterson, I turn my attention toward the East Passaic yearbooks, and that's when I'm hit so hard by what's staring me in the face, I nearly fall over. Why didn't I do this sooner? I begin a frantic shuffle through the stacks until I find what I'm looking for: the East Passaic High School year book from 1964—the year of death listed for the local Sy Goldberg we found in the death registry. I flip to the *S*s and there he is: Sy Goldberg! Next to his name are the usual clubs and honors one sees in a yearbook write-up—National Merit finalist, National Honor Society, Latin Club, Future Business Leaders of America—but underneath his name is the word "deceased" and the years of his birth and death. Sy died while he was in high school! Then I flip to the front of the yearbook, and there, in the *A*s, is Giovanni Amato—future corrupt mayor.

The mayor *knew* Sy. He also knew that he died before he had a chance to graduate high school, go to college, and, most important, hold a job. That last fact making Sy a perfect candidate for identity theft.

I close the yearbook and run straight to the city desk and Harry.

chapter twenty-one

Scooped!

I arrive on Friday morning armed with cleaning products and rubber gloves, prepared for day three of my battle in dust-bunny hell.

"I can't believe Harry's making us finish the library," I say.

"Who else is he going to get to do it?" AJ asks.

I shrug. I'm a tad miffed that Harry didn't grant us a reprieve after my yearbook discovery on Wednesday, not to mention all the extra research AJ and I did yesterday. We located Sy Golberg's original obituary on microfilm and found out that his father died when he was a baby. Sy's mother, who never remarried or had any other children, died a few years after her only child. So sad.

"I dunno. I just figured we'd be helping out with more important stuff until Michael gets back. We're both sort of in on this story now, aren't we?"

"Okay, two things here," AJ says. "Number one, I don't think Harry and Michael need help strategizing from a sixteen-year-old intern. And two, I don't want in on it."

"Then why did you agree to follow the mayor with me all those times?"

"For a smart girl, you really don't get it, do you?" And then he snaps open the newspaper so I can't see his face.

I'm about to react to what he just said when I catch a glimpse of the front-page headline, and my mood goes from annoyed to outraged. MOTORCYCLE GRANDMA HITS THE ROAD. Underneath is a photo of Tessie, the Harley-riding, Avon-selling woman I met at the deli, sitting on her pink Hog. The byline underneath the photo? Tony Roma.

"That a-hole stole my story!" I scream. Harry, Alice, Rocco, and Jack all stop what they're doing and stare at me. Without thinking, I grab the paper away from AJ.

"Sam," AJ says softly. "What up with the 'tude?"

I point to the front page. "This story? The motorcycle grandma?" I whisper-scream. "*I* told Tony weeks ago that I wanted to ask Jack about doing a profile on her. I just . . . haven't gotten to it. But that's not the point. The only reason he even knew about her was because of me."

"Let me remind you, Coma Boy's a douche bag. I said it from day one."

At that point, Harry rolls himself backward in his chair and stops at the obit desk.

"Everything all right over here, D'Angelo?"

"Yes," I say. I'm no tattletale.

"Just checking," he says, and rolls himself back.

I want to cry, but no way will I let that happen. That jerk's not going to make me embarrass myself again. I know I don't have to prove that I'm a better writer and reporter than Pretty Boy, but I'm going to. I reach into my bag to pull out a pair of rubber gloves and Clorox wipes.

"I'm going to work on the library." I tell AJ. "I need time alone, to think."

"About what?"

"Stuff." That's what I say out loud to AJ, but what I'm really thinking is, *Revenge.* Tony's lucky he's still on vacation.

By Monday, I'm still not over Tony stealing my story, but I'm feeling better. A weekend off is just what I needed. I've come to my senses about putting itching powder all over Tony's desk chair and Krazy Gluing his phone receiver to the base. Anyway, I don't have time for negative energy. Michael's coming back from vacation today, and he and Harry are going to decide what to do with Sy's yearbook photo.

"I could go for Chinese today, Sam. Whataya think?" Jack says.

I'm passing around lunch menus while I wait for Michael to arrive.

"Sure," I say. "AJ can drive me over to pick it up when he gets here."

Two more weeks and I'll be able to drive myself. AJ will be relieved. I'm about to spread the word that I'm taking orders from Sunny Garden when I turn around and see Shelby standing right next to me. I stifle a gasp.

"What are you doing here?" I ask.

"Nice to see you, too," she says. "My mom dropped me off. I thought we could do lunch."

"I can't. I'm taking food orders, and AJ isn't here to help. Why didn't you call and let me know you were coming?"

"Because you would have said you were too busy for lunch. Anyway, I wanted to see where you work. Come on, you must have time for a salad or something."

"I told you, AJ isn't here yet."

"AJ has arrived," I hear a voice behind me say, and turn to see a smiling AJ.

"Hi, I'm AJ," he says, extending his hand.

"I'm Shelby. I came to take Sam out to lunch, but she says she's too busy."

"You should go," AJ says. "Take a real lunch and get away from this place for once. You've earned it after last week."

AJ is being nice. Shelby too. But her unexpected arrival is making me uptight.

"Okay, thanks," I say. "I'll be back soon."

At this point, I just want Shelby out of the newsroom— my newsroom—as fast as humanly possible. It feels like those times when I was little and my mom or dad would show up early to pick me up from school.

"Come on," I say, grabbing my bag and phone. "We can walk to the deli down the street."

"Aren't you going to show me around?" she asks.

"Look around," I say, grabbing her by the shoulders and rotating her. "This is the newsroom. Pretty basic as newsrooms go."

"Stop rushing me."

"Let's go," I say, trying not to give away the urgency in my voice.

"Fine," she says.

"Nice meeting you," she says to AJ.

"Nice meeting you, too!" he says. I squint at him.

We cross the Nerf court to the side door and are about to make it safely outside when who should we run into but Tony Roma. Back from his vacation and sporting an Aruban tan so dark, he looks like a gleaming pair of blue eyes. My anger over the motorcycle grandma story resurges.

"Whoa! Sorry, Sam and friend," he says, shifting his heavy laptop bag out of the way just before it body-checks me in the left hip.

"Hey, Tony," I say, and keep moving.

"So, you're the famous Tony," I hear Shelby say behind me, and turn to see a grin on Tony's face to rival AJ's.

"I didn't know I was so famous," he says.

"I'm Shelby. I'm taking Sam to lunch."

"Nice to meet you," he says. "I'm glad you're taking her out. She's here almost as much as Harry."

"Yeah, we should get going," I say. "I don't want to leave AJ by himself for too long."

I'm holding the door open with my back, willing Shelby to move through it with her flip-flops, toe ring, and short shorts when Tony decides he has one more thing to add.

"Hey, Sam, you should bring Shelby to bar night sometime. If you girls don't think hanging out with a bunch of old people is too boring."

I'm stunned into silence. Inside, I am frantic to break the eye contact between Shelby and Tony and cover up the fact that I never told Shelby about bar nights.

"It sounds like fun," Shelby says.

"You'll have to ask Sam what she thinks about Wednesday nights at the Harp."

"Okay, will do," Shelby says.

Inside the stairwell, Shelby pinches my arm really hard.

"Bar night? You never told me you've been going to bars since you started working here. And here I was thinking you were just working late all those Wednesday nights. Some friend you are, keeping a bar that serves minors a secret."

"I don't know if the Harp & Bard serves minors," I say, rubbing my arm. "And anyway, you know I don't really like drinking."

"Well, you know I do."

"It's no big deal, Shelby. Maybe you can come next time or something," I say, hoping I don't have to follow through.

The short walk to the deli makes me hot and cranky. I

wanted Chinese food today. I wanted to eat my steamed vegetable dumplings in the conference room with Meg and Jack and AJ and Grace, just like I always do. Shelby's intrusion is ruining my day.

"So, what's the deal with AJ? Did you ever find out if he's dating Jessica Palladino?"

"No," I say. I remember Jessica being all flirty with AJ the weekend of the Fourth. AJ was smiling at her the way he smiled at Shelby just now.

"Why don't you flat out ask him? Unless I'm wrong and you're not interested in him. Are you?"

"Jessica hasn't called the obit desk lately, but that doesn't mean there isn't something still going on there," I say, maybe more to myself than Shelby. "I don't want to pry."

We arrive at the deli, and I pull open the door with its jangly sleigh bells.

"Hi, Sam," John says from behind the counter. "Did you call in an order?"

"Hi, John. No, I'm eating here today with my friend. John, Shelby. Shelby, John."

"Nice to meet you, Shelby."

"Hi!" she says, giving him a cutesy wave.

We place our orders and sit at a table for two.

"So we're going Wednesday, right?" Shelby asks as soon as we sit down. "My mother can drive. We can pick you up and go straight from work. And she won't mind coming out late to pick us up—you know her. Or maybe Tony or AJ can give us a ride home."

I grind my teeth and think of Tony's demise.

Anthony "Tony" Roma, a competent feature writer known to everyone but himself as Coma Boy, died Monday. He was 19. Roma fell into a vegetative state (adding a prophetic effect to his secret nickname) shortly after returning from a ten-day vacation on Aruba, thus learning the hard way that, yes, there is such a thing as "too tan."

chapter twenty-two

Crosswords

On Wednesday night, Shelby and I walk into the Harp & Bard. I'm wearing the clothes I wore to work, but I did apply makeup and took some extra time on my hair this morning in anticipation of the outing. I blew it out and am wearing it long. When I see Shelby in her turquoise halter top and denim miniskirt, however, I don't know why I bothered. Even if I did look good this morning, eight hours in the newsroom has taken its toll on my appearance.

It never seemed like a good idea to bring Shelby to a bar night, and my fears are confirmed the second we set foot in the Harp. My high school life, like a deadly asteroid, is colliding with my newsroom world. I have been working with these people for weeks, and suddenly, it's like Shelby's assuming ownership. Without warning, she walks right up to Tony, who's standing at the bar talking to

Alexis, and says, "Remember me? I'm Sam's friend." I do admire her nerve; it's something I never would have done. The dirty looks from Alexis don't deter her.

"Who's that?" I hear Harry ask Meg.

"Sam's friend," Meg says.

"*Really?*" Harry says, not bothering to hide his surprise.

I guess maybe we do look like an odd pair. I'm happy to see AJ over by the jukebox and walk in his direction.

"No practice tonight?" I ask.

"Our singer's away."

"I thought you'd have better things to do, like go out with your girlfriend or something."

"You're joking, right? I told you Jessica isn't my girl-friend. She's not even around anymore."

Maybe I sensed this, but his confirmation seems important.

"Anyway, bar nights are lame. But a bar night with your wacky friend—this could be interesting."

"You didn't think she was so wacky when you met her on Monday," I say, my jealousy rising as I remember his silly grin.

"What's that supposed to mean?"

The next thing I know, Shelby is next to AJ and giving him a sideways hug!

"Hi, AJ," she says.

"Hey," AJ says back. Clearly uncomfortable. "I'm going to get a drink. Anyone want anything?"

Shelby opens her mouth and I cut in. "Nonalcoholic."

"Oh," Shelby says. "No thanks, then. I'll ask Tony to get me something."

WTF? "I'm going to get a Diet Coke," I say. I follow AJ and expect Shelby to do the same, but she's beelineing for Tony again, like a riptide I can't control. Is this about scoring beer or Tony? She knows how I kinda felt about him, until he stole my story.

Alexis is at the bar when we get there, holding out her money for the bartender. She looks in our direction and says, "It's like Chuck E. Cheese's in here tonight with all the kids around." Bitch.

There's a restless, uncomfortable energy in the room tonight. Or maybe it's just me. I talk to Michael for a while and see what's happening with the mayor, Sy Goldberg, and the yearbook picture.

"We're deciding how and when to confront the mayor with the yearbook picture," Michael says. "Absent any definitive evidence from city records, we've got to tell this story a different way and still make sure we're covering our bases and not slandering anyone."

"Got it," I say distractedly.

Ordinarily, I'd be much more interested, but I'm torn between doing what I want to do and hovering over Shelby, who is now playing the vintage Ms. Pacman machine with Tony.

Twenty minutes later, I lose track of her completely. I've been sitting with Meg and Harry. Shelby came up to me a while ago and said she was going to the ladies' room, but she should have been out by now. Looking around, I notice Tony is missing too, and more important, so is AJ. I push my chair away from the table and stand up while poor Meg is in midsentence.

"Are you okay?" Meg asks. "You don't look so good."

"I'm fine," I say. "I'm going to the bathroom."

There are two stalls inside. One normal-size, and one wheelchair-accessible. Hesitantly, I peek under that latter one, half expecting to see two sets of feet, but the bathroom is empty. Is that how I picture my best friend? What's wrong with me?

I'm walking out of the bathroom when I run into AJ.

"Hey, Sam. I was looking for you. I wanted—"

"Have you seen Shelby?"

"What? No. I wanted to ask you. . . ." He keeps talking, but I'm so focused on finding Shelby. "What are you doing?"

"Looking for Shelby."

"She's a big girl. She's not lost."

I scan the main barroom. It's not very big, but I still don't see her anywhere. I start walking away, and AJ touches my elbow lightly.

"Where are you going? I was trying to say something here."

I relax my tense shoulders and make eye contact. "I'm sorry—you're right. What were you saying?"

At that very moment, the back door swings open, and Shelby walks through, laughing, as Tony holds the door open for her.

"Where the hell were you?" It comes out angrier than I intended.

Shelby looks hurt. "I was just outside the door, talking to Tony."

"Why couldn't you talk in here?"

"It's my fault," Tony says. "I stepped outside to have a cigarette."

"You smoke?" I ask.

"Only when I drink."

"Speaking of which, I'm going to the bar," Shelby says, and then she looks at me. "It that okay with you, *Mom*?"

"Fine," I say, crossing my arms.

When I look up, AJ's stance is mirroring my own. "What?" I snap.

He looks like I just slapped him. "Why are you so pissed at Shelby?"

"Because I couldn't find her."

"Is that why? Or is it because of who she was talking to when you did?"

"What's that supposed to mean?"

"It means why do you care if she talks to Coma Boy?"

"Why do *you* care if I care?" I say.

Our eyes connect, and we just stand there—deadlocked. Anyone watching us might think we're having a moment, but I can read the anger in AJ's eyes and feel the negative tension between us. Why is this happening? I don't like him being mad at me, not tonight. Not ever.

He throws up his hands in disgust. "You know what? I don't. In fact, I'm out of here."

"AJ, wait—" But it's too late. In one angry motion, he's gone and I'm talking to a slamming door.

Meg finds me crying in the bathroom. "What's up, kiddo?"

It takes me a nanosecond to spill. "AJ's mad at me."

"Why?"

"He thinks I'm jealous that Shelby's been talking to Coma Boy all night."

"Are you?"

I shrug. "Honestly, I'm confused about that myself."

"Yeah, well, don't be too hard on your friend. Coma Boy has that effect on women. What's the big deal?"

"I guess the big deal is, that Shelby knows that at one point I was sort of crushing on Tony."

"Are you still?"

"I'm over it. Especially since he stole my story."

"He stole your story? You never told me. Which one?"

"Motorcycle Grandma."

"Ah. That did seem too clever to come from him."

"Right?"

"Maybe you should tell him how you feel."

"Who?"

Megs puts a hand on my shoulder and looks me in the eye. "I can see why AJ's getting frustrated."

I give her a guilty grin. "Thanks, Meg."

"Anytime."

When I go back into the barroom, Shelby is holding a beer and talking to Tony and Alexis. Interesting. Alexis has never said more than two words to me. I don't want to be here anymore, and it's probably a good idea to leave before Shelby gets drunk and embarrasses me in front of my coworkers.

"Hey," I say when I walk up to Shelby. "We should get going."

"Noooww?" Shelby whines. "It's still early."

"Hang out awhile longer. I can drive you girls home," Tony says.

"That's okay," I say. "We've got a ride."

"You go if you want to. I'm staying," Shelby says.

"Can I talk to you a minute?" I say to Shelby.

"Go ahead and talk. I'm standing right here."

I clench my fists.

"Fine. I'll be sitting with Meg and Harry," I say, but then I lean in close so only Shelby can hear, and whisper, "Enjoy your first and last bar night."

It produces the desired effect. Fifteen minutes later, we leave the Harp & Bard and suffer through a wordless car ride home. When we pull up in front of my house, I thank her mom as I'm getting out of the car.

"Bye," Shelby says.

"See ya," I say back.

Somehow I knew, as I slammed the car door shut, it was the last thing we would say to each other for a while.

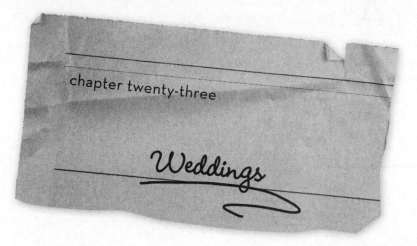

chapter twenty-three

Weddings

Thursday morning at work I spend hours rehearsing an apology to AJ in my head. By noon, I'm feeling anxious that he still hasn't shown up yet. I hope he's okay.

"Hey, Alice," I say. "Did AJ call in sick today?"

"He took some time off, remember? He won't be back until Wednesday."

That's right. He mentioned driving out to Ohio with his dad for his cousin's wedding. I forgot it was this week. Shoot. And I'll be off Wednesday. It's my birthday, and I'll be taking the road test to get my license. I won't see him until Thursday. That's a whole week.

"Don't worry," Alice says. "You'll do fine by yourself."

"Thanks, Alice."

Alice was wrong. I'm not fine by myself. More like uptight, angry, and unfocused. The sight of Tony Roma makes me want to puke. It's not easy to avoid him since we all work together in one newsroom, but I do my best. Thursday and Friday pass by more slowly than eight hours of standardized testing. I spend most of my time polishing up my story on Mr. Kovalevsky, the POW. I want it perfect before I turn it in to Harry.

"Nice job, D'Angelo. You should be proud," Harry says when he finishes editing it. "It's going to run in Sunday's paper."

Harry's words should have me turning cartwheels, but there's this tightness in my chest that hasn't left since my fight with AJ at the Harp. Not even the sight of my name on the front page of the Sunday *Herald Tribune* is enough to snap me out of it.

"Fantastic story, sweetie," Mom says over breakfast.

"You must have worked hard on this," Dad says.

"I did. Thanks." I don't look up from my cereal.

"Anything you want to talk about?" Mom says.

"Just tired."

This prompts her to get up from the table and feel my forehead, first with her palm, then with her lips.

"You've been working too hard," Dad says.

"Maybe," I say. "I'm going to go lie down for a while."

I can feel my parents looking at each other as I clear my dish and leave the room.

On Sunday afternoon, I decide to walk down to Bargain Books & Beans—not for research, just for me. I'm too unsettled about my lack of communication with AJ (and to a lesser extent Shelby) to worry about stupid Sy Goldberg and the mayor. I take my laptop and a copy of the paper with me.

"Sam!" someone yells when I walk into the coffee shop. "Over here!"

"Hey, Joanne," I say as she waves me over.

"Great story on the POW," she says, pointing to the copy of the *Herald Tribune* in my hand.

"You read it? Thanks," I say.

"Listen, I've been wanting to talk to you about something."

"Okay."

"I've decided to join the dance team this year," Joanne says. "I've been dancing at the same studio since I was three, and I finally feel confident enough to compete on stage, in front of people. So I'm going for it."

"That's wonderful, Joanne. You should!"

"Anyway, I don't think I'll be able to handle competitive dance and being yearbook editor. So I wanted to ask if you'd be interested."

"That's so nice of you to offer, but what about Missy or Sarah? I wouldn't want to step on any toes. And wouldn't a faculty adviser have to approve me or something?"

"Missy and Sarah are too busy with sports, and I've already mentioned your name to Mr. O'Hara. He thinks you'd be perfect."

"He does? Wow." Mr. O'Hara teaches AP English. He's also yearbook adviser. "Can I think about it?"

"Sure. But I hope you say yes. You can totally handle it. The hardest part is making sure everybody sticks to the word count when they write their blurbs. I know it's hard, since you don't get to say much about your time in high school in less than a hundred words."

"So true."

I buy an iced latte and chat with Joanne some more before she leaves. I'm happy I connected with her and Fiona's group this summer. I've known them since middle school, but for some reason, we've never really talked. Maybe Shelby's right about my tendency to be standoffish.

I open my laptop and think about Joanne's offer. What she said about editing students' blurbs made me think of obits. What doesn't? But it also gives me the perfect idea for my blog. I type the first sentence:

Imagine you've been asked to write your own obituary. What would it say?

The rest just seems to flow from there. I talk about obits and high school yearbook write-ups and how we tend to look at our lives more closely when we're aware of the limits—word counts, space, time. And then I tell the story of Anton, the boy who died in the fire. When we are gone, what words will we leave behind? That's when a name for a blog hits me, Dead Lines: A Teen Obit Writer's Take on Life. When the time is right, I'm going to show it to Harry and see what he thinks. Writing about the dead this summer has taught me how to live. Maybe I've got something to share. I wish I could show this to AJ.

I pick up my phone and text him.

Hey,

I say. My temples pulse as I wait for his reply. I try to look at my computer screen, but my eyes won't focus on any words. The same thing happens when I scan the coffee shop and the sidewalk outside: I don't *see* anything. Finally, my phone makes a text sound.

Hey,

AJ replies.

I'm sorry.

I type back immediately,

U should be,

and then, two seconds later,

☺

Then I type, C U soon? A few minutes go by before I get a return text. I laugh out loud when I see it. A photo of him from the nose up, like he's peering into the camera. The attached message says,

Sooner.

The tightness in my chest loosens, and for the first time since bar night, I can breathe.

———

Tomorrow is my seventeenth birthday. My insides feel like a shaken bottle of soda that needs to settle down before it explodes. Summer is coming to an end, and the sun is already setting earlier. I need to get a run in before it gets too dark.

I set off toward the high school so that I can run laps around the track. When I reach the parking lot, I again hear the familiar sounds of the marching band on the practice field. This time, however, I also hear a coach's whistle. The football team is in the stadium. Ugh. I'll have to run laps while the team conducts its practice drills. Do I really want to sweat in front of all those jocks? Screw it. I want to run around the track, and I'm going to run around the track. I up the volume on my iPod and go for it.

Mile One: Shelby and I haven't spoken in seven days, and there's no real reason why. We aren't mad at each other,

are we? The problem is, with every day that goes by, there's
another day of silence between us.

Mile Two: If she had called, I would have talked to her.
Why hasn't she called me? Why haven't I called her?

Mile Three: Tomorrow I'm going to tell Joanne I want
the job as yearbook editor.

Mile Four: When I get back to work, I'm going to show
Harry my sample blog idea.

Mile Five: I wonder if I can get into Columbia or NYU
if I apply. New York City is a lot closer than central Pennsyl-
vania. I could keep working at the Herald Tribune *straight*
through college. Maybe I should dust off my SAT prep book.

Mile Six: I keep running. And running.

I arrive back home just as the tangerine-colored sun
sinks below the horizon. I shower and get ready for bed.
But even after watching five different shows involving culi-
nary competitions—cupcakes, wedding cakes, five-course
dinners—and finishing *Waiting for Godot*, I can't turn my
brain off. Work, school, college, Shelby, Coma Boy, AJ.

It's three in the morning, and I'm lying in bed, willing
myself to fall asleep. My pillow feels too hot. I keep flipping
it to the cooler side, but it's no use. Finally, without stopping to think, I grab my cell phone and dial the one person
I want to talk to right now.

"Hey," he says.

"You're home?"

"I'm home."

"How was Ohio?"

"Flat. Far."

"I'm glad you answered your cell."

"I left it on. I was hoping you'd call."

"You were?"

"Yup."

I spit it out before I lose my nerve.

"You know, there's this amazing band playing at the Jersey shore the Friday before Labor Day," I say.

"Are you asking to be my plus one?" AJ asks.

"I am."

"That's more than two weeks away."

"I wanted to give you time to think about it."

"Pick you up at seven," AJ says.

"It's a date."

"Is it?" AJ asks.

I think it is.

chapter twenty-four

Advice Column

Today is my birthday. It began like all the others for as far back as I can remember—with my dad singing that Beatles birthday song. *"Bananananana. You say it's your birthday."*

"It never gets old," Dad said this morning.

"Yes. Yes it does," I told him. "But thanks."

Mom and I had to cut him off after the third line.

Since Dad has a meeting in Manhattan, Mom took the morning off to drive me to the Division of Motor Vehicles for my road test.

Despite that Mr. Harrison at the DMV said my parallel parking "left a little to be desired," he was feeling generous and passed me anyway. At long last, I'm a licensed driver in the state of New Jersey.

"Congratulations, honey!" Mom says, and gives me a sideways squeeze when we get in the car. "You keep your eyes on the road, and I'll text your father to let him know the good news. We'll all go out tonight to celebrate. Your choice."

Twenty minutes later, I drop my mom at the bus stop, and for the first time ever, I'm alone in the car. It's a bit odd, lonely even. At home, now that the road-test anxiety and excitement are behind me, I have nothing to do. Shelby and I had always planned on celebrating after my road test (provided I passed) with our first car ride together alone. One of those stupid rites of passage we've been dreaming of ever since I got the Barbie Volkswagen Beetle and Shelby got the RV. But there's been no call or text from Shelby. Part of me was hoping my birthday would be the icebreaker.

I return a birthday text message from Meg and tell her I got my license. Even Joanne remembered, and I mentioned it only in passing that day at the coffee shop. When I text back my thanks, I add that I want the yearbook-editor gig.

YAY! ☺ Will let Mr. O'Hara know.

I'm going to be yearbook editor! This calls for a snack. I'm craving pretzels dipped in cream cheese. There's nothing better than the salt-dairy combo. At nine fat grams per two tablespoons, however, I usually opt for fat-free cream cheese, which is merely a white substance for people with good imaginations. But screw it, today is my birthday and I'm going for it.

"Get your shoes on, birthday girl!" Gram says. She's standing in the kitchen with her pocketbook draped over her forearm. "You're taking me to IHOP for lunch."

"I am?"

"Of course! I've been waiting for this day for a long time. I'm free of Aunt Connie."

Okay . . . *still* not how I envisioned seventeen to be, but it's got to be better than watching daytime TV and hearing about yet another drug that may cure my horrible disease but brings on dry mouth, insomnia, suicidal tendencies, chronic diarrhea, and a limp.

"Just let me grab the keys."

"Now you're talking."

An hour later, Gram is sitting across the table from me at IHOP, a heaping pile of chocolate-chip pancakes with extra whipped cream in front of her. My phone rattles on the table. A text from Shelby.

Well? Happy Bday. Miss u!

"Hmm. Nice of her to finally remember," I say.

"Shelby?" Gram asks.

I nod.

"What's going on with you two?" Gram asks.

"We're not talking," I say.

"Why?"

"I'm not exactly sure. It's not like we got in a fight. More like we got on each other's nerves, big time, the night she came out with my newsroom friends."

"I see. Is a boy involved?"

"Sort of."

"Is he worth losing a friend over?"

I guess that would depend on which boy we're talking about.

"I guess not," I begin. "It's hard to put into words. First she was talking to Tony, then AJ, then Tony again. She was being . . . *Shelby*."

"And you were probably being *Sam*."

"What?"

"Look, I don't know exactly what happened, but you should still talk to her. Don't let twelve years of friendship end because of one bad night."

"Okay, but let's say your best friend flirted with Gramps."

"Your grandfather was a handsome man. Women flirted with him all the time."

"And?"

"And maybe it was my fault for not making a move sooner."

"It took you ten years!"

"Exactly! Learn from my mistake. Come on," she says. "You mentioned your grandfather, and that gave me an idea. Let's go pay him a visit."

She grabs the check and slides out of the booth. Gram's right. I've already taken care of the first part—making a move (at least I hope AJ perceives it that way)—now it's time to take care of the rest. Before we leave, I text Shelby.

Thx! Got it! TTYL.

When we get to the Glendale Cemetery, Gram and I walk down a small, grassy hill before we reach Gramps's grave. I notice Gram's name is already on the headstone, alongside her date of birth. It would freak me out to stare at that blank space, where my date of death would someday be engraved. It doesn't seem to bother Gram, though. Neither does the fact that my grandfather is not actually *here*. Gram talks to my grandfather as if he's standing in front of us, leaning against his headstone with his hat in his hand.

"James!" she yells, as if he's merely on the other side of some bad cell-phone reception. Gramps's name is Vincenzo, but she uses "James" because when he started school, it's what his teacher called him. "I brought Sam here to see you. It's her birthday! She's seventeen now—can you believe it? She got her driver's license today. She's so smart and beautiful. You would be very proud."

"Gram," I say, embarrassed, but not sure why.

"I miss you, you know. I still reach for you at night sometimes, but you're not there. But don't be sad about that or anything. I'm no spring chicken. I'll see you soon enough." Gram pauses, and I'm not sure where she is going with any of this.

"Maybe Sam wants to talk to you now. Do you? I shouldn't put her on the spot. Let's give her a minute," Gram says. "Go ahead," she whispers.

I'm not sure I can talk aloud to my grandfather with my grandmother standing right there. I don't know what I'm going to say or if I'm going to say anything, and then, much to my own surprise, I just start talking.

"Hi, Gramps. It's Sam. Sorry I didn't come to see you sooner. I'll visit more now that I've got my driver's license. And I don't know if you know this, but I've been working at the *Herald Tribune* all summer, writing obits. I'm starting my senior year soon. I'm going to be yearbook editor, and I'm excited about that, but nervous about all the rest. Shelby and I have been drifting apart. Shelby's the same old Shelby, I guess. But these past few months . . . I'm different. It's like, in the newsroom, I matter. That's why I'm so upset with Shelby. It was never about some boy. It's like she tried to ruin my place. Can friends be jealous of each other and still be friends? That's probably what I need to figure out."

Phew. Well, who needs therapy when you've got a granite headstone? Gram stands beside me and takes my hand. Without speaking, we stare straight ahead at Gramps's grave like we're watching the credits roll at the end of a movie. It feels like Gramps is staring back.

"I love you, Gram," I say.

"Oh, you're just saying that because now you're afraid *I'm* going to die." Then she says, "I love you, too."

"You're just saying that because you want me to drive you around now," I say.

"Maybe," she says, and winks.

Before we leave, Gram bends down near the headstone. She makes the sign of the cross and then gently runs her hand along the smooth surface next to her name.

"Are you afraid?" I ask.

"Of course not. I know your Gramps is on the front porch."

I imagine heaven, for Gram, is a house. Inside the house are her brothers and sisters, her mother, and the father she lost when she was just a little girl. It's always Sunday there, fried meatballs bubbling in tomato sauce on the stove, Italian music on the radio. Inside the house, there is lots of talking and laughter. Outside, Gramps is waiting for her to come home.

———

Before we leave for the restaurant, my parents give me my birthday cards and presents. (No car, but I didn't expect one.) I got an amazing sapphire-and-diamond ring in white gold. "It's beautiful," I say when I open it.

"So are you, Sam. We thought so on the day you were born, and have every day since," Mom says, all teary.

"Seventeen is a special birthday," Dad says.

"For me, too," Gram says. "Sam's my new ride."

In addition to a check, Gram gave me a gift card to Pit Stop gas.

We have dinner at Amici's, my favorite restaurant. Mostly, it's been a nice birthday. I feel guilty, though, because even though my family is great, part of me longs for what I imagine to be the typical birthday for a seventeen-year-old girl—roses from a gorgeous boyfriend, dinner at some romantic restaurant, hearing the words "I love you" for the first time—and not from a blood relative. I've been waiting all day to hear from AJ. I thought after our phone call last night, things were fixed between us. More than fixed. Progressing.

When we turn onto our street, Mom says, "Looks like you have company."

AJ's Jeep is parked in front of our house. My hand is already on the door handle. It's all I can do to not leap out of the moving car.

Standing in the driveway, I make the introductions, and AJ shakes everyone's hand. I wonder if Gram gives him an extra squeeze. I can tell by her sly smile, she's already got a crush on him.

"I came by to see if you want to go for a ride," AJ says. "But I don't want to interrupt anything."

"Go ahead," Dad says.

Mom just nods and smiles.

Gram gives me a thumbs-up when AJ turns the other way.

I'm getting into the passenger door when AJ hands me the keys.

"Here, Miss Daisy. Why don't you drive me for a change?"

I take the keys and smirk.

"You did get your license, didn't you?" he asks once we're inside.

"I suggest you buckle your seat belt," I say as I turn the key.

"Wait," AJ says, when I'm about to shift into drive.

"You're not having second thoughts are you?" I kid.

"Funny." He plugs his tunes into the car stereo. "I didn't have a chance to get you a birthday present with Ohio and all. I considered a Buckeye travel mug, then I thought, What *is* a Buckeye, anyway? So I made you this instead." He holds the screen in front of me.

"'Sam-I-am'?" I read.

"Hit play," he says.

We drive along with all four windows down. It's already dark, and there's the faint scent of fall in the mid-August air. The songs AJ picked for me range from college radio to classic rock, and I try to discern if there's a common thread, some message behind his choice of music for me.

"I love this," I say. "Thank you."

I'm smiling so big, my cheeks hurt. His eyes cut toward me, and he looks uncomfortable as the next song cues up. Acoustic guitar. Male vocalist. I'm trying to place the mellow, baritone voice.

"Is this Jack Johnson?"

My remark invokes AJ's incredulous face. "Where'd ya get Jack Johnson?"

I listen to the words, about a girl who's shy but strong, hasn't yet figured out where she's going, and doesn't know the power of her words. The boy in the song says he's known from the start she's something special. At first I think the chorus is *"Everything she says."* But then I listen more closely and realize he's saying *"Everything Sam says."*

"Oh my God! This is you!" My mouth is so dry, my lips stick to my teeth. "I didn't know you could sing and play guitar."

AJ grins. "Don't forget 'writes songs.'"

"You wrote me a song? This song is about me?" My vision blurs. I take the next right turn too sharply, roll over the curb, and nearly hit a mailbox.

"Steady, Sam-I-am," AJ says, putting a hand on my shoulder. I've got a death grip on the steering wheel, but what I want more than anything is to throw my arms around him.

"Uh, how 'bout we switch places?" AJ suggests.

"Done," I say.

I pull to the curb and park. Our doors swing open simultaneously, and we both walk in front of the Jeep. Our paths are about to crisscross as we head to opposite sides, but then I grab AJ's hand. We are standing face-to-face in the headlights' glow. I move to give him a hug. He moves, I think, to kiss me. I tilt my head toward him. Can this finally be happening? Suddenly, the Jeep starts rolling backward.

"Crap," AJ says, running toward the open door and leaping into the driver's seat.

A few hours later, around midnight, I call AJ from the house phone. I left mine with him so he can upload my playlist and my song.

"So, your car's all right?"

"It's fine. I forgot to tell you to use the emergency brake."

"I'm so sorry."

"*I'm* sorry."

"For what?"

"Not letting the Jeep go."

My cheeks and neck are on fire, and my heart is pumping in double time. My body is obviously telling me how much I like him, so why aren't the words coming out of my mouth? *Say it, Sam, just say it!* My mind screams.

"AJ?"

"Yeah?" he says, lowering his voice.

"I know how we can help Michael get his mayor story."

"Of course you do. And here I thought you were going to talk dirty to me."

Me too.

chapter twenty-five

Police Log

On Wednesday, I pull into the bank parking lot, keeping a safe distance from the mayor's car. AJ and Michael are in the back seat. A photographer named Lane sits up front with me.

"Okay, this is it," AJ says when the mayor exits his car. "Just like we planned."

"Should I go with Sam and AJ?" Lane asks.

"No," Michael says. "You and I will go in the back door now and try to get some audio and photos."

"Got it," Lane says.

We all exit the car at the same time, a slightly nerdy vice squad, and head for the bank. Inside, the mayor is standing at the counter where the blank deposit and with-drawal slips are, filling something out. AJ and I pretend to do the same on the opposite side of the bank. Michael and Lane stand near the entrance, looking at bank brochures.

We all close in when the mayor approaches the teller's window. "Hello, Mr. Goldberg," says the friendly teller I spoke with last time.

Michael and Lane stand in line behind the mayor, within earshot. It's time for me and AJ to do our thing.

"Mr. Goldberg, Mr. Goldberg," I yell.

The mayor whips his head around. "Do I know you?" he says.

I go with the excuse I used the first time.

"We just started working at Bargain Books & Beans. Your daughter said you'd be able to cash our paychecks for us since we don't have accounts yet."

"What? How did you two know where to find me?"

Michael speaks up from behind him. "Because we followed you, Mr. Goldberg."

The mayor spins around at the sound of Michael's voice. Lane snaps photos as Michael continues talking. "Care to tell us why the mayor of East Passaic banks here as Sy Goldberg?"

Michael whips out a photocopy of Sy Goldberg's yearbook picture. "Look familiar? Remember your old, *deceased* classmate?" Lane keeps clicking.

The mayor doesn't answer. Instead, he pushes past Michael and Lane and hustles toward the back door. AJ, Lane, and I go after him while Michael stays inside and starts asking questions. Once the mayor's through the back doors, he starts running. The three of us stand on the sidewalk and watch as he jumps into his luxury car and speeds away.

———

Five days later, Michael's story takes up the entire front page of MONDAY's paper:

WHO IS THE REAL SY GOLDBERG?

That's how the headline with a point size of around seventy-two reads. Underneath are two photos: one of the mayor at the bank, the other of Sy Goldberg, taken from the 1964 East Passaic High yearbook I found.

Michael worked for more than a week, conducting interviews and writing the main story. He also did a piece on identity theft.

"Bless my tabloid heart," Harry says, holding the paper at arm's length and gazing at the front page like it's a newborn baby. "This is a fine start to my Monday morning."

"Yeah, the tellers and bank manager gave me some great quotes about how they knew the mayor as Mr. Goldberg," Michael says.

"I like the interviews you did with Sy's old classmates who remembered the day he died in the car crash," I say.

"Good job, all," Harry says. "Now get me my follow-up story on Kiki Ramirez."

Most identity thieves use stolen Social Security numbers to open credit card accounts, take out loans, and steal cell phone service. The mayor's scheme to put dead people on the payroll and collect their salaries was slightly more ambitious.

We're sharing all our information with federal authorities, and hopefully, on the day the mayor walks out of city hall in handcuffs, the *Herald Tribune* will still be in business and Michael will be there to cover it.

"It's a shame Bargain Books & Beans will probably close. I've grown to like that place," I say to AJ and Michael. "Guess the mayor's daughter is going to have to find either a new calling or someone to bankroll her coffee shop *legally*."

"You rock. You know that, don't you?" AJ says. He grabs my hand and gives my fingers a light squeeze. Friday can't get here soon enough.

"Group hug!" Michael yells, and throws his arms around both of us. "The Harp tonight?"

Sy Goldberg died today, again. May he finally rest in peace.

"D'Angelo, catch!" Harry yells before slamming me in the back of the head with the Nerf basketball.

"Come on, you two," Harry says to me and AJ. "I'll play you both at once and still win."

"You're on," AJ says.

I don't know how to play basketball. It's not a sport for the altitude challenged. I must look like an idiot, running around the newsroom floor, arms flailing, waving to AJ to pass me the ball. But who cares? I'm having a great time. Harry does indeed beat us, but not before I make one spectacular basket. AJ and Harry are shuffling around near the net. I go long or far or away from the basket—whatever it's called in this game. AJ passes it to me. I jump and take a shot from about ten feet away. It arcs up high and goes right in.

"That's what *I'm* talking about!" AJ yells, and then gives me a high five.

———

Shelby calls the obit desk that afternoon. We haven't seen each other since that bar night, but at least we've been texting and talking.

"I read the story today," she says. "You're like Peter Parker."

Spider-Man's alter ego was a news photographer, but I don't correct her. She's trying.

"Wanna do something after work today?" she asks.

"I can't, I'm getting my hair done. I've got an appointment with Meg's stylist."

I imagine I hear Shelby falling out of her chair.

"What are you getting done? Don't cut it—you have gorgeous hair."

"I don't know. I'm thinking about dying it red."

"Okay, okay. I can see that."

"Want me to stop by when I'm done?" I ask.

"I'd love that," Shelby says.

It will be good to see her. The dynamic between us is changing, but it's a good thing, I think, for both of us.

———

Meg's stylist, Jimmi, gives me the star treatment. When I get there, he kisses me on each cheek, European style. Then he has someone fix me a sparkling water with lime as he sits me down at his station. Above his mirror I notice a plaque that says YOU ARE MY HIDING PLACE.

"I got them from a customer," Jimmi says when he sees me looking at it. "She says she comes here to escape her life for a while."

"I get that."

"You have beautiful hair," he says, pulling the back out straight and studying the color.

"Meg thinks I should dye it red," I say.

"What do you think you should do?" he asks.

"Definitely leave the length," I say.

Jimmi shows me a color chart, and we discuss the option of highlights, but in the end, I decide on a mere trim, a little product, and a blowout. Jimmi turns me toward the mirror. It's funny, I'm actually startled by my own reflection. My first reaction is, *Who is that pretty girl?* Jimmi looks worried by my lack of immediate response but relaxes when I break into a nearly giddy grin.

"That's me!" I cannot stop smiling.

"It sure is. Gorgeous."

chapter twenty-six

Stop the Presses

It's still dark when I pull into the *Herald Tribune*'s parking lot on Wednesday morning. Spaces are scarce. I find a spot in the last row. I take a deep breath and get out of the car. Crickets are chirping away in the skimpy shrubbery lining the parking lot. Moths and mosquitoes swirl around in the streetlights. It's like I'm going to a funeral. In a way, I guess I am.

As I walk toward the building, John from the deli down the street pulls up next to the side entrance in a white van. He rolls down the window. "Hi, Sam," he says. "Harry asked us to cater a breakfast for your shindig. Came in early to help him out."

"Wow. That was nice."

"Can't say no to Harry."

Don't I know it. When John opens the van's back doors, the scent of bacon wafts toward me. Maybe today won't be so bad after all. Bacon makes everything better.

I step into the newsroom at 4:50 a.m. I don't think I've ever seen it this packed. There are some dudes in suits gathered in front of Harry's office, by Alice's desk, and Bernadette is back! Harry emerges from his office sporting his office-casual look, with one addition—a black armband. He's carrying a small cardboard box, too. I'm not surprised when Harry reaches in and pulls out clumps of black armbands, the kind professional athletes wear to symbolize a fallen team member. He passes them to Meg and to the reporters who sit across from her. "Here, put these on. . . . Sam!" Uh-oh. I make a beeline for him, and he hands the box off to me. "Pass these out."

We are all about theatrics today.

As we begin filtering into the press room, the enormous machines, which I now know are outdated, are still running. The front page and three others are passing overhead in big sheets. *Chug, chug, chug.* Like it's taking its last breaths. The death rattle. No wonder the press guys wear soundproofing headphones. Harry assembles everyone near the control panel, where, predictably, there's a green on and red off button. Harry waits for a signal from Franco, who's standing a level above us, leaning over a rail and watching the paper go by for the last time. He gives Harry a thumbs-up.

"That's it," Harry says. My throat tightens at the sound of those words. I don't know why I'm getting so emotional. Harry walks over to the control panel. I assume he's going to hit the red button, but he says something to Dan, who then walks over to the wall, where there's a red button with a softball-size circumference that says EMERGENCY—it's almost cartoonish.

Dan smacks the button, and the machines grind to a halt.

"I've always wanted to do that," Dan says. And then he wipes his eyes with his thumb and index finger, a quiet motion that is duplicated by more than half the people standing in the room.

"Dan, Franco, and Henry. Come up here. I'd like to say a few words," Harry says.

"These are the men who have been putting the ink on our paper for at least three decades. The ones who work through the night so a newspaper comes out each and every morning. They were here through eight presidential elections, Vietnam, the day John Lennon was shot, Nine-Eleven, two wars in Iraq, and the same number of space-shuttle disasters. They helped us chronicle local events and world history. They are the *Herald Tribune*'s soul. We owe these men a round of applause."

With that, the room erupts. Tears stream down my face. I'm not alone. Even AJ's eyes are watery behind his glasses.

———

I go for a coffee run at three o'clock—maybe my last. When I come back, the newsroom is eerily empty. AJ's at his desk, but that's it.

"Harry wants to see you in the conference room, right away," AJ says.

"Am I in trouble?"

"Well, all the dead people on today's obit page are in fact dead, so I'd say you're probably safe," he says with an AJ-like smirk. "Nice hair, by the way. I meant to say it earlier."

I touch the top of my head. I'm surprised he noticed. "I just got a trim."

"I know."

Tentatively, I make my way toward the conference-room door and step inside, expecting to see angry Harry. Instead I'm greeted by a chorus of "Surprise!!!" The whole newsroom is there—even Bernadette stuck around. There's a sheet cake on the table.

"It's a going-away party and belated Happy Birthday all in one," Jack explains.

"Wow," I say. "Thank you all so much. I can't believe you did this for me."

"Don't flatter yourself, D'Angelo," Harry cautions. "We did this because we like cake."

The icing reads HARK, THE HERALD ANGEL DRIVES!

"It's all spelled correctly, Moronica," Bernadette snarks. "You weren't here to write it."

"I'm glad you're back to proof it," I say, and smile.

"Only part-time," Bernadette adds. "And my doctor says no more burgers."

She's looking well, rocking a lilac tank top and

matching eye shadow. Slimmer even. The sight of her makes me remember the beginning of the summer, before so much of everything happened. I'm just happy she's still breathing.

"We also made you this," Grace says.

It's a framed copy of my POW feature story.

"You can show it to your kids someday. Tell them it's how people used to get their news before we all got chips implanted in our brains," Jack says.

"This is amazing. Thank you," I say.

"D'Angelo," Harry says, "try getting some work done after you have your cake. I want to see you in my office before you leave today."

I notice Tony exiting with Alexis on his heels. A perfect pair. Without either of them in the room, I'm able to enjoy my big piece of fattening cake with my friends.

When we're back at the obit desk, AJ asks, "So, is this really your last day? What did Harry say when you showed him your blog and told him about your idea?

I'm tidying my desk and packing up my personal stuff. I open the top drawer and take out a file folder filled with my clips.

"He said he'd read it and get back to me. Between the mayor and the presses shutting down . . ."

I trail off. My voice is on the verge of cracking, and my eyes are getting watery. AJ changes the subject.

"So, Friday?"

"Friday," I say. "Finally."

"I'm out of here. I've got to meet with my adviser to get some classes changed," AJ says. He puts a hand on each of my shoulders and looks down into my eyes. "Call you later?"

"You better."

———

It's four thirty when I sit down in the chair facing Harry's desk. I've been here for nearly twelve hours.

"You've done a great job this summer," he says. "I wanted to talk to you about your blog idea and your request to stay in the fall."

I don't like the sound of this.

"Given the events of this morning, even with all the restructuring, the future of the paper is shaky at best. Layoffs are imminent, and I don't know that we'd be able to pay you. Your senior year is an important one. I don't want you wasting your time here if we don't have much to offer."

"That's okay, I don't need the money. I can be an unpaid intern or work for credit or something. It wouldn't be a waste of time, really. Before I started working here, I felt . . . People here get me. I get them. I need this place. . . ."

My voice cracks. I thought I could do this without getting emotional. Harry senses it. He clenches his jaw and looks out the window.

"Tell you what. I like your high school blog idea. I do.

Maybe it can be a weekly thing on our website. And if you really can't live without the obit desk, and you don't mind working for credit instead of money, we can probably use you around here a few hours a week. Especially since Coma Boy is leaving and I'm moving AJ to features. As long as the paper stays in business, we'll always have a place for you."

"You mean it?!" I spring out of my chair and plop back down again. I'm more excited to hear AJ's moving to features than I am to be staying.

"There's something seriously wrong with you, D'Angelo. But it makes sense. That seems to be the general theme around here."

"Thank you, Harry. So I'll see you Monday after school?"

"No, you won't. I want you to settle in to school first. Get more ideas for your blog. Whip that yearbook staff into shape. Be the first to figure out what the next big trend is going to be, or start your own. Go out with a bang, not a whimper. Get it?"

"I get it," I say. And I do. T. S. Eliot and all.

"One more thing," he says, opening the top desk drawer to take out a small, wrapped package. "It was Meg's idea to get this for you."

I unwrap my gift. It's a digital recorder. On cue, Meg leans her head into Harry's office.

"Like it?" she says.

"Love it," I say. "Just like you guys."

"All right, get out of here, D'Angelo. Enjoy what's left of

summer. We'll see you back here in two weeks. Be prepared to kick some ass."

"Okay." I'm about to leave, and then I don't think—I just act. I run up to Harry and throw my arms around him. It is a softer hug than I expect. He pats my back, and I can feel a summer's worth of experiences passing between us.

"Sit down, D'Angelo," he says. "Hands on the desk."

I do as he says. He takes a rubber stamp and ink pad from his drawer and plops an armadillo on each hand. "Now get out of here, for real."

I make my rounds and say my good-byes—or see-you-soons, as the case may be—and when I finally leave the building, I'm feeling lighter. The bright sunlight feels right for late summer. The sky is a pure, hazeless blue. I can sense autumn behind the white, puffy clouds. The first day of school is only a few days away, and for once, I don't mind.

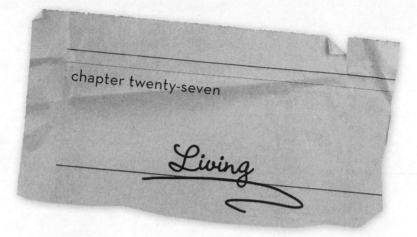

chapter twenty-seven

Living

My mom gets home from work early and finds me staring at a mound of clothes on my bed that I've deemed totally unacceptable. It's everything I own.

"What's up?" she says, surveying the garment explosion.

"Is it okay if I stay out later tonight? I'm going to see a band."

"With *who*?"

"AJ."

She's all teeth. "My daughter is dating a drummer."

"Okay, do not get goofy on me. I need something that makes me look like a pretty rocker chick."

My mom doesn't miss a beat. She steps out into the hall and screams down to my father.

"You're on your own for dinner tonight! Sam and I are going to the mall." Then she turns to me and says, "Grab your stuff."

———

Three hours later, I'm sitting in AJ's new vehicle. "Is this a hearse?" I ask as I fasten my seat belt. He never mentioned he was ditching his Jeep.

"A very old one. I thought it was cool. Perfect for hauling gear."

AJ is looking at me—at every inch of me. I should be enjoying this moment more, but I can't seem to get past the fact that I'm riding in the front seat of a hearse. Better here than in the back, I guess.

I'm wearing my new low-rise jeans with the blown-out holes in the knees. My mom also talked me into a tank top with a built-in bra that is certainly giving me a boost, as well as black wedge sandals that are doing the same. I'm almost hot. And I can tell by AJ's sideways glances as we pull away that he thinks so too.

My dad says that the best live music is usually found in the worst parts of town. That thought immediately pops into my head when we double-park in front of the bar to unload AJ's equipment. It's on a corner next to an abandoned warehouse and across the street from a bus terminal. A large bouncer sits out front, propping the door open with his stool. AJ shimmies in the front door sideways, lugging the bag containing his kick drum, and says, "Hi, Dave. This is Sam."

"Hallo, Sam," he says, and for a split second, I think he's doing a fake English accent.

"Hi," I say.

"I need to see some ID. It's all ages tonight, but you've got to get a wristband if you're old enough to drink." The accent has not been dropped and I realize he is, in fact, English.

"I'm not." I hand him my license anyway.

"So I see. You're barely seventeen."

"Like the white-winged dove," deadpans AJ as he scoots past to get the rest of his gear.

"Ah, Stevie Nicks," Dave says. "You're too young to know who that is."

"I *love* Stevie Nicks. My father—"

"Plays in an eighties cover band," finishes AJ as he lugs his kick drum into the bar.

I find a seat at the end of the bar, closest to the makeshift stage, which is merely a drum riser built on milk crates and tucked into the corner. The stage lighting is band provided and accomplished by clamping two lights with colored cellophane to each PA speaker pole. There are four other guys in AJ's band—two guitarists, a bassist, and a lead singer. When they finally start to play, I'm immediately sorry I didn't bring earplugs. They're incredibly loud. I recognize a few songs from my iPod playlist, but there're just as many I haven't heard. Still, they pull me in. Crunchy guitars, heavy bass, hard-hitting drums—their sound fuses hardcore and melodic rock, like the Warped Tour bands that all the skater kids like.

AJ plays the drums like he feels it—every beat, without

even thinking about it. If he's counting in his head, it doesn't show. His movements are fluid and intuitive, his drumsticks a mere extension of himself. His style isn't flashy. I wouldn't have expected him to be a show-off, anyway.

His face exudes a combination of happiness and intensity I've never seen in him before. He is where he needs to be to play his part in this song. And just when the song hits its groove, when the guitar, bass, drum, and voice are all moving like one big whole, he looks up and smiles, first to himself, then at me. Then he does a roll, and it's back to eyes closed.

My own failed attempts at learning to play an instrument have only heightened my appreciation for what musicians do and the places a band can take me when I'm lost in their sound. I'm in one of those places now, oddly relaxed sitting by myself amid a mostly male crowd that's here for the music, not Jell-O shots. I'm also diggin the way AJ's legs look in those jeans, especially where he's got a big midthigh tear. I'm mesmerized by that spot as he pounds the kick drum with his right foot and keeps time with the left.

Anthony John Bartello, drummer for the Grammy Award–winning band Love Gas, died Thursday. He was eighty-seven. AJ, as he was known by friends and fans, is survived by his wife of fifty years, Samantha (née D'Angelo) Bartello; two children, Alfonsina ("Ally") and Neil; and three grandchildren.

But the vibe is broken when Rob McGinty walks in with Liza and their crew. Shelby's guy, Mark, is here too, followed by Quarters dude, Josh. Speaking of Jell-O shots . . . they all look like they've walked into the wrong bar. Perhaps they were looking for the Tiki-style establishment, frequented by MTV reality "stars," farther down the coast. It's possible my presence would have gone undetected, but Rob spots me and, for some reason, decides to come up and say hello. Must he always be so nice? Liza and her cronies hang by the door, looking as if they believe they'll get their summery ensembles dirty if they venture any farther into the club. They're all less than ten feet from where I'm sitting, but a parallel universe away.

"Hey," Rob says, taking a few steps toward me and giving mc a half wave. "You here for the band?"

Love Gas starts another song, and I have to yell to be heard. "I know the drummer."

"Nice," Rob says, looking around uncomfortably. "Mark pumped gas with the guitarist this summer."

Like a dog who hears his name, Mark appears at Rob's side along with Josh.

"Look who it is," Josh snorts, loudly. He sounds drunk. "Shelby's friend."

"This is Sam," Rob says.

"Here with all your friends tonight?" He leans too close to my face, and I have to arch my back against the bar to avoid his beer breath.

"Chill," Rob says. He attempts to pull Josh away from

me, but not before the six-foot-five wall of Dave arrives. Bouncerman. A new kind of superhero.

"These guys bothering you, Sam?" he says, bumping up against their backs. "Is there a problem here?"

"There's no problem," Rob says. He and Mark move drunken Josh toward the door. They stay until the end of the song, and then they leave en masse. I feel kind of bad for Rob, but I guess that's the price he pays for choosing to hang around with people like that. It would be hard to date Rob knowing his friends are part of the package. Sometimes not getting the guy you wanted since sixth grade can be the best thing that ever happened to you.

———

"Thanks for your help tonight," I say to Dave when the set is over and Love Gas begins packing up.

"Anytime," he says. "The jocks and frat boys always make my night more interesting. Douche bags, all of them."

After we finally get into AJ's hopefully *temporary* vehicle, he pops out one last time to open the back door. I hear him unzipping a canvas bag, which I hope contains gear and not a body. When he comes back around to the driver's seat, he has a small, square box in his hand with a bow on top.

"I almost forgot to give this to you," he says.

"For me?" I ask.

"No, for the other girl I'm driving home tonight. Yeah,

you," he says. "Sorry it's a little late. Happy birthday, Sam."

It's like I'm watching this happen to some other girl.

"But you already gave me a gift. The playlist, the song—"

"Just open it," he says. "I suck at wrapping, so I skipped that part."

I flip open the box, carefully part the tissue paper, and pull out delicate silver earrings, which at first glance appear to have two sparkling charms—one on each earring. Then I take a closer look.

"Are these armadillos?"

"I know they're unusual, right? But, I don't know, I saw them and thought, 'Sam.'"

"They're perfect," I say, because they are. I touch them lightly with my index finger, then turn and give AJ a slightly awkward hug.

He breaks free and holds my face in his hands. My breath catches in my throat.

"You're so pretty," he says.

And then he kisses me softly on the lips, once, before pulling back. Chills run down the back of my neck. I look into his eyes, and I realize he is waiting for me to say something, but I decide the better answer is to just kiss him back. Then I move my lips along his jaw and up to his ear. "I wish we had done this sooner."

"The band or the kiss?"

"Both."

"I was waiting for you to get real about Coma Boy."

"And I was waiting for you to define what Jessica was to you."

"I told you. She wasn't my girlfriend. Nor was she ever going to be."

"Why?"

"Because something happened right after I met her."

"What?"

"You walked into the newsroom."

I tilt my forehead against his and look into his eyes.

"So, does this mean I'm not your latest I-don't-know?"

"You're my Sam-I-am," he says.

I look down at the tiny open box in my hand. Armadillos. They *can* explain everything.

The ride home is quiet, except for the music from AJ's various playlists, but somehow just being together is comfortable and exciting all at the same time. AJ holds my hand the entire time and doesn't let go until we pull up in front of my house.

"See you tomorrow?" I say.

He puts his hand behind my head, leans over, and kisses me again.

"It *is* tomorrow," he says.

He's right. I open the door but then quickly slam it shut. In one impressively smooth motion, I slide across the leather bench seat and settle into AJ's lap. Our lips meet just as his arms wrap around me. Every cell in my body feels alive. I'm exactly where I want to be, and who I want to be.

Acknowledgments

It takes the time and talents of many to turn one writer's ideas into a book. I am so very grateful to the following people.

My incredible agent, Kerry Sparks, for believing in this novel from the start and sticking with me through every draft. Every writer should have a Kerry in her corner.

My editors, Eve Adler and Christy Ottaviano. Their decision to acquire this novel was life changing, and their editorial guidance and input elevated the manuscript on many levels. I am so thankful to Christy, my kindred spirit in all things pop culture, for pushing me (gently) to discover the story I truly wanted to tell. Thanks to Kathryn Little and everyone at Henry Holt/Macmillan and Christy Ottaviano Books, especially Amy Allen.

My amazing family, who have always given me the love, support, and encouragement to pursue my dreams— even the crazy ones. My parents, Grace and George Salvato, my sister and brother-in-law, Melissa and Anthony Collucci, their children, Anthony James and Cassie, and my other parents, Dolores and John Doktorski. I love you all.

My best friend, rock, and better half, Mike, and our beautiful daughter, Carley. Every day, they inspire me to do everything better.

My talented and generous critique partners, Karen Cleveland, James Gelsey, and Sharon Biggs Waller. Special thanks to Lisa Anne Reiss, who told me before we'd even met she had a feeling this book was going to sell, and Melissa Eisen Azarian, whose eagle eye and attention to detail always make my manuscripts better.

My NHS girls, for getting me through high school and for their continued support.

Former Greenwillow editor and present editorial consultant extraordinaire Sarah Cloots, who was the very first person to request my full manuscript. (I kept the e-mail.) Thank you for seeing something in this novel when it still had a long way to go.

My very early readers and dear friends who suffered through that first draft yet still gave me the encouragement I needed to turn those pages into a novel: Adriana Calderon, Liz Davis, Eddie and Laura Konczal, Michele Russo, and Christa Conklin.

The members of the real Love Gas, Chris Wargo (lead vocalist/guitarist), Eric Kvortek (guitarist), Austin Faxon (drummer), and Mike Doktorski (bassist/husband).

Special thanks to all my friends and colleagues past and present in the news biz, who continue to inspire me and helped make the plot and newsroom scenes more authentic, especially Ted Anthony, Lisa Colangelo, Pasquale

DiFulco, Allison Inserro, Bob Sullivan, and my first editor, Walt Herring, who is no longer with us but by most accounts was a newsman's newsman.

And finally, in memory of Lisa Kamm, my first cousin and friend. You are loved and missed.